THE BROKEN SWORD

The Broken
Sword

A MARY FOX
ADVENTURE

Jonathan Posner

Winter & Drew Publishing

Contents

3rd Edition
Published by Winter & Drew Publishing

1st Edition published as
Mary Fox and the Broken Sword
December 2020

THE BR♦KEN SWORD

A MARY FOX ADVENTURE

1

CHAPTER ONE

I had to act quickly, or the well-dressed man lying on his back would be skewered with the sword. Another man with the look of a brigand was standing over him, weapon poised, ready to plunge it into the helpless fellow's chest.

The would-be victim saw me and his pleading eyes met mine across the forest clearing.

Letting out the loudest yell I could muster, I urged my horse to a gallop.

The brigand looked up and I could see his eyes widen as I thundered towards him. I must have been something of a surprising sight; my hair loose and flying out behind me; my plain chemise tight across my chest and my men's breeches tucked into my brother's black leather boots. I dare say he had never seen such a girl before, and certainly not one so intent on riding him down.

He scarce had time to raise his sword before I was on him,

knocking the weapon from his hands with my horse's hooves and leaping across the man on the ground as if he was but a low fence on my father's lands.

I wheeled my horse, Hestia, round hard and brought her to a stop. This tight manoeuvre made her rear up and let out a piercing neigh as her front hooves lashed out furiously, stopping the assailant from running forward to retrieve the sword. I glanced quickly round. It must have flown across the clearing when I had charged; I could see it shining in the sunlight close to a tree just behind me. He was brave, I will give him that, but Hestia's hooves were a fearsome barrier and he could not get too close.

Hestia dropped to the ground, so he took his chance and started to run forward. I realised I could not let him get back his sword, so, taking a deep breath, I let out another fearsome yell, pulled at Hestia's head once again to make her rear up, then threw myself backwards from the saddle and rolled to the ground. Now I was standing behind the rearing horse. I turned and picked up the sword in a single movement and held it out before me.

Hestia dropped again to the ground and ran forward. The brigand must have seen his chance. He rushed around her and came towards me with his eyes down. I assume he was seeking out the sword on the forest floor. Then he glanced up and checked as he saw that I had already retrieved it – and I was holding it out before me.

But it was too late. With a sickening jolt and a sound like sodden clothing falling to a stone floor, he ran straight onto the sword and impaled himself deeply upon it. I screamed as his contorted pock-marked face came up close to mine, and the feel of his hot, sticky blood covered my hand. I shall never forget the sight of his eyes boring into mine with a burning look of shock and pain, before they suddenly went dull, like a candle He snuffed out, and rolled up into his head. With a sigh, he dropped to his knees, then fell to his side on the ground with the sword still sticking out from his chest.

The whole thing had taken less time than a hawk flies a hundred yards.

As I stood panting, with my bloody hand held away from my body, the man who had been at the brigand's mercy raised himself from the ground and stood. He walked over to me and stopped.

He looked me up and down, then shook his head as if in disbelief.

"A mere slip of a girl, and you have saved my life," he said slowly. "I would not credit the bravery of your action this day." He went down on one knee, and took my hand – thankfully the one not covered in the brigand's gore – and kissed it. "I am forever in your debt, mistress."

"Please," I said, now feeling embarrassed, "it was nothing. I only did what anyone would have done."

"Nay," he answered. "Few men would have done so, let alone a girl. You saw I was at that fellow's mercy, and you understood my need. You showed the resource and courage of a man, and a man twice your age at that."

He stood up and kicked the body over onto its back, then put his foot on the chest and pulled the sword out. It came free with a gruesome sucking sound that made my stomach churn and bitter bile rasp at the back of my throat.

He wiped the sword clean, using the corner of the man's

jerkin, then stood tall and stared down at me. He was not a young man; there was much silver in his hair and trim beard, but he carried himself with the easy grace and poise of a practiced soldier. I could see by the colour and material of the clothes he wore that he was a noble of some description – most probably a knight – and this was confirmed when he spoke again.

"Sir John Fitzwilliam, at your service, mistress." He bowed low.

I knew that manners required me to curtsey in reply, but I decided not to do so. This whole scene was outside convention – perhaps it would have made me seem weakened. I could hardly play the demure young lady while I had a bloodied hand and the body of my victim lying by my boots. I stood as tall as I could and replied, "Mary Fox, stepdaughter of Sir Andrew Fox, of Marchington Manor."

"Then I must thank Sir Andrew for the good fortune his stepdaughter has brought me," he said. "Are we far from Marchington Manor?"

"Yes," I said, just a little too quickly. It must have sounded false and he raised an enquiring eyebrow. "It is some days' ride from here…" I added, trying to retrieve some credibility but only making things worse. He raised his eyebrow even further, now clearly disbelieving. I took a breath. I supposed it would have to come out sometime – it might as well be now. "In truth, I have… run away from home," I said quietly.

"Ah ha. I see." He stepped back a pace and studied me again. "My duty would always be to return a runaway girl to her family." My face must have fallen, for then he smiled. "But in this case, the girl in question has just shown amazing bravery and saved my life. So today," his smile broadened, "I shall not do my duty, but I shall offer the girl in question my protection." He put his hand on my shoulder, and I felt a sudden rush of warmth towards him, as I imagined a girl should feel towards a fatherly older man.

Would that Sir John were my father, instead of the cold, unfeeling taskmaster that I had run away from.

He took his hand away and glanced down at the corpse at my feet. "Although after the way you disposed of this ne'er-do-well with his own sword, I feel I should be seeking your protection on my quest, Mistress Fox, rather than offering you mine."

"Nay, sir, it was but a happy accident that the brigand ran onto the sword."

"Aye, but you came upon the scene and made to run him down, then leapt across my prostrate body with such style and grace, then did a truly acrobatic exit from your horse's back and landed squarely on your feet. 'T'was a wonder to behold."

"Your quest?" I asked, trying to take the conversation away from my supposed prowess and back to something a little more comfortable.

"Aye, I am on a quest that means much to my family." He paused, looking me up and down. Then nodded, as if concluding a debate with himself. "You are welcome to join us if you have no other plans?"

Without a moment's pause I found myself nodding and smiling in agreement – surprising myself with my willingness to throw in my lot with this total stranger. But then, why not? He had looked at me and had seen someone with whom he wanted to share his journey – why should I not return his trust? I had run from home, away from my overbearing step-father and the plans for my life that would have surely killed my spirit – why not throw in my lot with this kindly knight and aid him on his quest?

Perhaps I could learn from him how a father was supposed to behave towards a young woman? Or must I continue my journey alone – a journey that in truth had no other aim than to get away from Marchington Manor? No, this seemed like a good decision.

Had I but known the danger and adventure that lay ahead, I might have thought differently. But at the time, I simply said, "Aye – I will join you and help where I can."

"Good," he said. "Then you had better have this." He held out the sword, hilt facing towards me. "It is a good weapon – like as not the brigand took it from a fine gentleman in the course of his evil activities."

I reached and took the sword, hefting it in my hand. It felt light and natural, as if the sword was an extension of my own arm. I tried a few practice swings and lunges, moves that my brothers had so studiously taught me.

Their secret lessons had been something of a diversion for them, almost as an amusement to keep their little sister quiet. But I had dedicated myself to the learning and had proved myself as a model pupil, until I could turn their swords on my own with practice and ease. They had professed themselves surprised, then impressed, and finally, proud.

And now I had killed a man.

"There – a born swordswoman indeed," Sir John said with satisfaction.

I smiled. A swordswoman! Whoever heard of such a thing in the realm of King Henry, Eighth of that name?

I decided to change the subject – there was something he had said earlier that I had not understood. "Us?" I asked. "You said 'us' when you talked of your quest. There are others on your journey?"

"Aye," he said ruefully and called out, as if to the forest in general, "Robert! Robert! Come here boy! Come out!"

I looked round cautiously – wondering who he was summoning.

"Robert, you useless fool, you can come out of hiding now. The thief is dead and with luck we will have back our property!" Sir John looked around. "You would have left me to die at his hand!" he shouted. "But this woman here has more bravery in her little finger than in all of your mangy carcass, and she has saved me!" He stared from tree to tree around the clearing. "Oh, by the Risen Christ boy, show yourself!"

There was a pause, then a shadow moved slowly from behind one of the trees. As Sir John and I watched, a young man stepped slowly out into the clearing. He was maybe my age, maybe a year or two older, with sandy hair, a wispy beard and pinched, thin features. His ornate doublet, breeches and sleeves were in Tudor green slashed with red. His grey hose ended in fine black shoes.

"I am sorry, Father, I panicked and I hid. I am sorry." His voice was high and querulous, and I could not believe that he was sorry at all. I decided that this cowardly young man, who would have let his father die, would need to work very hard indeed to earn my trust on whatever journey lay ahead.

"Aye, well, you are no swordsman. God only knows what

you would have tried to do, anyway," said his father, with what I thought was an unnecessarily forgiving tone. "I was only fortunate that Mistress Mary Fox came by in time to dispatch the thief to meet his master Satan in Hell, which is where he belongs."

Robert looked at me, taking me in with wide eyes and, I think, some trepidation – as if I were a Knight Errant stepped straight from the tales of ancient heroes. Then he looked down at the brigand's body at my feet and the sword I carried, and he paled to the whiteness of freshly cleaned linen.

Sir John gave a snort of disapproval, then marched over to where a small covered cart was standing under a tree, with an elderly-looking horse between the traces. I was surprised to see it there – in the action of that morning I had simply not noticed it. "This is what we have sought these two long weeks," he said over his shoulder. "I would to God our property is in here."

He pulled open the small latched door at the back of the cart, then leaned in and rummaged around. After a few moments, he emerged triumphantly, holding a leather bag about the size of a wooden trencher dining plate. "I have it!" he yelled, like a small boy in his excitement. "This is what we have been seeking since the godless thief took it from us some two weeks since!"

He fumbled with nervous fingers at the cords that tied the top of the bag. Finally he got them undone, then opened it and looked inside.

He broke into a delighted grin, and it was if the bag contained a powerful light that cast a golden hue across his smiling face. He reached carefully inside and took out what looked like the golden hilt of a sword, encrusted with rubies, emeralds and other stones. It seemed to light up the whole clearing and turn it to gold. I was surprised to see that there was only about six inches of blade attached, ending in a jagged cut that itself glinted in the sunlight through the trees.

He held it up triumphantly.

"Once more it is ours! Once more I hold the Broken Sword!"

2

CHAPTER TWO

We carried the body of the brigand into the deep forest; me and Robert carrying a leg each and Sir John with his arms hooked under the man's shoulders. On Sir John's command we swung once, twice, thrice – and flung the body away. It flew across some low bushes and landed with a loud crash out of our sight.

"That is good riddance," observed Sir John with satisfaction. "I warrant no person will mourn his passing, but belike the birds and the worms will welcome it."

I shuddered at the thought of this nameless man laid to rest under the sky without any benediction, and the birds picking him apart. I muttered, "May God have mercy on his soul."

"I doubt the Lord will trouble himself with this one," said Sir John cheerfully, as he walked back through the forest. "He was a rascal who lived outside the laws of God and man alike. The world is a better place now you have removed him from it."

"I would not have done so by choice," I said. "It is a sin to kill."

"Aye," he said. "That it is." He stopped and looked me up and down. "But there may come a time when you have to kill again, Mary. Be ready for it."

"I will do all I can to avoid it."

"That is all well and good." He walked on. "Although it may not avoid you. Be aware of that."

I followed Sir John out into the clearing. "You must tell me your story," I said, changing the subject to something more comfortable than killing. "How did this thief come to have the Broken Sword? How did you track him and find him? How did he overpower you before I rode by?" I stopped, as another thought came into my mind. "And what is your quest, now that you actually have it back?"

"Questions, questions, my dear Mary!" he laughed. "All will be told when we are settled together and we have eaten." He walked over to the little wooden cart.

I realised Robert was not with us and I turned to look for him. At first I did not see him in his green clothing against the all the trees and leaves, then I made out the red slashes of his sleeves, and from that the shape of him. He was quite a few yards away, facing back into the forest by a tree, and I could see from the way he was standing that he was relieving himself against its trunk. As I watched, he finished his bodily function, restored his clothing and turned round. Seeing me staring at him he stopped, and for a moment we faced each other in icy stillness.

Standing there with his sandy hair and skinny body in green and red clothing with black shoes, I could not help but think he looked exactly like a spindly plant that grows out of the low bushes on the forest floor.

Not a good plant – what he put me in mind of was a weed.

I decided that henceforth he would be called Weed.

With a low chuckle, I gave him a cheery wave – which only made him scowl at me, then I turned back to the clearing and walked over to the rickety wooden cart.

Sir John had his head and upper body buried inside, throwing its contents out over his shoulder. A threadbare blanket, some aged pots and pans, a mouldy hunk of bread and a blackened leather drinking costrel flew out and landed behind him. He came out of the cart and leant down to pick up the costrel. He shook it curiously then undid the stopper, tipped it up and shook it again. No liquid came out. He put his nose to the neck and sniffed, then made a grimace and threw it down.

"Empty of water and stinking of putrefaction," he said. "Of no use to us at all."

"I have a costrel with wine, plus some bread and ham in my pack," I said, looking to where Hestia was nibbling on grasses at the edge of the clearing, with my small pack of provisions and some changes of clothing hitched behind her saddle.

"Aye, and we have much the same on our horses, that are tethered nearby," he said. "I was curious to see if there was anything we could take off this brigand that would add to our provisions before we find ourselves an inn." He turned back to the cart. "I still have a few more items to explore," he said, and once more disappeared into its interior. Further blankets and pans flew out, then slowly he withdrew again, turning to me with a smile. I looked at the sizeable leather purse he was holding. He hefted it with a wink, and the clink of coin sounded across the quiet clearing.

"I thought as much," he observed. "Such a thief and cutpurse as this would have gathered illicit coin much as a squirrel gathers hazelnuts." He hefted it again, then suddenly he tossed it across the clearing to where I was standing.

"Here, Mary Fox," he said, "take it, with my blessing!"

I caught it; it was heavy with coin. "No, I cannot," I said. "It is yours by right, Sir John. You have been chasing this man for two weeks."

"Then it is yours by conquest," he answered. "I chased him, but you killed him."

"No, sir. I cannot."

"So you have brought a fortune with you," he enquired impishly, "that you do not need more?"

"I have some coin," I said, "enough for my modest needs…"

"Then think of it as my gift," he said, with finality.

I realised I should give in with good grace. "Thank you, Sir John," I said, studying the purse. It was a strange piece, the like of which I had never seen before. It was made of soft tan leather, with a complex Saxon-style device branded onto it; a twisted, scrolling pattern that looked like two snakes inter-twined. It was tied with a leather thong, and there were two further loops of leather for securing it to a belt.

I turned to walk over to where Hestia was standing, and almost bumped into Weed. He must have just now come up behind me and had such a look of hatred on his thin face that I would burn in flames before him. Did he think that the coins should be his? Surely he would have realised that even the most forgiving father would scarcely reward cowardice? I smiled at him again, which caused him to glower even more, then I walked to my horse.

I was about to drop the purse into my bag, then I thought of the angry Weed behind me – perhaps as like to steal it? Instead I took out my own purse, emptied it into the brigand's, then fastened the new purse securely to my belt.

Why was I so compelled to tease this young man? It did not serve me well to be such a shrew to him, yet I found myself unable to stop. Resolving to try and be more forgiving, I took out my costrel and packet of provisions and walked back to the cart.

What food and wine we had was shared out as we sat in the clearing. Sir John's hearty appetite meant he had the lion's share, as Weed did no more than pick moodily at his food, and I have never been one to eat more than is required to stop my hunger. Indeed, it was one of my stepfather's constant complaints – that the finest foods would be presented to me and I would select only the tiniest amounts. But what should a girl do – eat so much of these rich foods that she must bring it all back later? I think not. She should have sufficient and she should eat it with modesty and dignity.

When we had finished, Sir John leaned back against the cart wheel and said "So, Mary Fox, you would know how and why we came to this situation?"

"Yes, I would," I answered.

"Indeed. But first I must tell you of the legend of the Broken Sword, for that is what lies at the heart of this story."

He settled back a bit more against the cart wheel, then cleared his throat, closed his eyes and began.

"The Broken Sword belonged originally to my great grandfather's great grandfather's great grandfather; a man named William who came from Skipton in Yorkshire. He was born around the twentieth year of the reign of the first King Edward, who was known as Longshanks, and he fought in the battle of Boroughbridge in the winter of 1322 under the banner of the loyalist Sir Andrew Harclay. Legend has it that William and his company of pikemen were being attacked on the bridge by the rebel forces under the Earl of Hereford, and at the height of the battle, William saw the Earl's banner coming towards them. He and a pikeman jumped off the bridge and hid underneath, and when the Earl crossed it on foot, William had the pikeman strike up through the timbers, killing the rebel Earl."

I caught my breath, imagining the horror of the Earl's death. "But what of the sword?" I asked.

"Yes, the sword." He paused. "The sword itself belonged to the Earl of Hereford, and as the pike entered his body, it was flung from his hand and fell to the bed of the river. William noted where it fell and was able to retrieve it after the battle. When he was later knighted for his loyalist support, he was allowed to keep the sword."

"But how came it to be broken?" I asked. "And why is it so precious to your family?"

"Yes, I have come to that point in the story." He opened his eyes and smiled. "So now I must tell you what happened more than twenty years after the battle of Boroughbridge."

Once again he closed his eyes. "By now William, or Sir William as we must call him, was living in a fine manor house he had built near Skipton, with his wife and three daughters. Two of his daughters were dutiful, respectful girls, while the youngest one, Matilda, was a beautiful but wayward child; impetuous and impulsive, and always a burden on the heart of her loving and forgiving father."

I envied Matilda – at least she had a loving and forgiving father. "What did she do?" I asked.

"For one thing, she had the gift of the sight – she could see things yet to happen and was known as a being possessed of some white magic."

"Witchcraft?" I gasped. He nodded. "Did the family accept her nonetheless?" I asked.

"Aye – they believed it was a gift not a curse."

"Indeed," I said. I knew such things were more accepted in the olden days than they are today – people now have grown afraid of what they do not understand and are as like to call in a witchfinder if a girl shows any powers. "But you say she was impulsive?" I asked. "Surely if she had the gift of sight, she would know the consequences of her actions?"

"So you would believe. But it seems she only had the sight when the spirit descended upon her in times of need or emergency. Otherwise she was an ordinary, if somewhat wayward, child."

"So what else did she do?"

He smiled ruefully – as if it were his own daughter he was describing. "One thing she would do was lead on the young men of Skipton in a most improper way – and that is how she got into trouble with the son of Jack Foley, a local ruffian.

Matilda gave Jack's son Rowan to believe she was sweet on him, and he decided that she was the one he wanted to marry. Of course, it was quite out of the question; William forbade it, and in truth, Matilda had no interest in the young man anyway. Rowan, however, was set on taking her for his wife and he brought his father in to make his cause."

Sir John paused, opened his eyes and took a swig of wine. I glanced at Weed – he was idly making circles on the ground with a short stick. No doubt he had heard this story many times, and it no longer excited him.

"Did the ruffian Foley cause trouble?" I asked.

"Indeed he did. He came to William's house and pleaded his son's cause most forcefully."

"What did William do?"

"As you would expect – William told Foley very clearly that he and his son must take themselves away, and that they were to leave Matilda in peace."

"And did they?"

"Nay. Two nights later, Foley, Rowan and five of their ruffian cohorts approached William's house, intent on taking Matilda as a prisoner for Rowan to marry. In the dead of night, they broke into the house. It seems they were making for the girl's chamber in order to carry her off – and if necessary kill all the family to get to her. But William heard them, quickly took hold of the Earl of Hereford's precious sword and stood in the hallway to prevent them."

"One man against seven?" I asked, aghast.

"Aye," answered Sir John. "But he had practiced many hours with the sword and he was ready."

A father prepared to die to protect his family! Oh, how I would love to have such a thing! "Did he fight well?" I asked.

"Yes, his blade moved faster than the eye could see; parrying, blocking, thrusting, sweeping and turning against each one as they came against him. He fought like a man possessed as he protected his family and his daughter, and soon all the men except one lay dead at his feet."

"All except one? Which was it?" I asked, although I had already guessed the answer.

"It was Foley himself," said Sir John, confirming my guess. "The two men squared up to each other; Foley, who now wanted nothing more than to avenge the death of his son and his men, and William with a family to protect from this murderous ruffian." Sir John took another draught of wine from his costrel, as he prepared to continue.

"They fought fiercely hand-to-hand for some time, but neither man could gain an advantage and both were tiring. Then something dreadful happened."

"What was that?" I gasped.

"William's sword had taken so many cuts and hits to its blade that it had become severely weakened – and when Foley made a wide sweep at William's side and William tried to turn Foley's blade on his, it split, leaving only the stump as you saw earlier."

"Oh no!" I cried. "Was William hit? Did he die?"

"Fortunately not. Foley himself stopped his fight for a moment – he was probably as surprised as William by the breaking of the sword – and before he could swing his blade again, William seized the moment. He leaned forward and swept the remaining part of the blade across the man's open throat. Foley went down like a felled tree and was dead before he hit the floor."

I shuddered again. "So the sword gave William victory, even though it was broken."

"Indeed it did." Sir John smiled. "Then William called the family to his side to celebrate the victory, but when she saw all the bodies, the spirit descended on Matilda. She went white, then as rigid as a plank of wood and spoke out in a hoarse, guttural voice quite unlike her own. She pointed at the bodies and said that death had visited the house and placed a curse on the family. Death or sickness would become a regular visitor throughout all the generations." He paused. "Unless…"

"Unless what?" I asked, my breath catching in my throat.

"Unless the Broken Sword is kept by the family at all times. With its protection, however, the curse would be kept at bay and the family would thrive."

"And did they thrive?"

Indeed they – or should I say 'we' did. The family prospered under the favour of both the local barons and the kings in London. Over the years we gathered many lands and great wealth and moved from Skipton to Suffolk; into a new manor house built near the village of Nacton. At times it seemed that the family's good fortune was more than just luck or endeavour; always it was put down to the presence of the Broken Sword, secured in pride of place on the wall of the Great Hall, above the high table."

"But then it was lost these two weeks," I exclaimed. "Has some tragedy befallen your family?"

It was Weed who answered, his high voice sounding

unusually flat. "Since it was stolen, my mother is fallen sick and my sister also. We fear they may die if it is not restored in good time."

"Oh." I was silent a moment, as I contemplated the personal tragedy that confronted these two men.

"We have also had much of our lands enclosed," added Sir John, "and are facing extraordinary rents we must pay to the Duke of Norfolk. So we are most likely facing financial ruin also." He rubbed his beard thoughtfully. "All of which started the very day the Broken Sword was stolen."

I could see that the Broken Sword was indeed a protection for the family from the curse. "How was it stolen?" I asked.

"The brigand came to the door, seeming to beg for alms," said Sir John. "My wife, Anne, is a kindly soul, and she went to fetch a coin. While she was gone, the brigand slipped into the house. He must have been looking for something to steal and found his way to the Hall. The Broken Sword, with its gold hilt and precious stones, would have been as a gee-gaw to a magpie, and he took the piece from its place on the wall. When my wife came back to the door with her coin, she saw him walking his horse and cart quickly away down the path. She went back into the Hall a while later and saw with horror that the sword was gone."

His voice broke slightly. "Shortly after that, Anne, and my daughter Margaret also, both fell into a drowsy stupor and would scarcely eat. Then we had the news about our lands and rents to pay. Robert and I immediately set out to find the brigand and return the Broken Sword, so we can restore our fortune and the health of my wife and my daughter. We tracked him from village to village these past two weeks, travelling many miles away from our home near Nacton – but each time we thought we had come upon him, we found he had slipped away. Then, this morning, we finally came across him, stopped here."

He stared unseeing across the clearing. I thought he must be re-living the dreadful events of earlier in the day.

"We quickly and quietly retreated, securing our horses out of sight, then approached again on foot as quietly as we could. We watched the cart for some time, but there was no sign of the man. Eventually, we decided he must have walked away, so we ran out into the clearing, intent on searching the cart. Unfortunately, he was hidden behind it, waiting – he must have seen us approaching earlier. We were caught by surprise, and before I could defend myself, he had me to the floor and was preparing to run me through with his sword. My son Robert..." he gave an accusing look at Weed, who had the grace to look ashamed "...decided to hide himself rather than save his father."

Yes, I wondered about that...

He turned his attention to me with a small smile. "So I was much relieved when a brave and resourceful young woman called Mary Fox appeared, saw my predicament across the forest, and ran the brigand down."

He paused. "The rest you know. We have the Broken Sword back again. At least it is in our possession. But we must get it back to our womenfolk as quick as we can, if we are to have any hope of stopping the curse taking its full effect – and restoring both them and our family fortunes to health."

He gave me a long, careful look; the smile suddenly gone.

"So we would have you join us on our journey home. It

is many miles back to Nacton and there will be any number of perils lying in wait, but if the resourcefulness and courage you have shown thus far is any guide, you will be a most welcome companion on this journey."

He looked at me in expectation, waiting for me to confirm once again that I would accompany them. I looked at Weed, who was scowling – a young man much in need of someone to teach him both manners and courage.

I looked at Sir John himself, a kindly man who seemed, even on an hour or two's acquaintance, to value me more than my own stepfather had done in all my life.

"Yes," I said, with more confidence than I felt. "Yes, I will."

"Good," he said. "But before we move one step from this place, Mistress Mary Fox, you will tell us your story."

3

CHAPTER THREE

The afternoon sun cast bright fingers of light down through the trees and into the quiet clearing, as I sat with my legs crossed on the dry earth. I took a deep breath. "I will tell you my story," I said, "but I would not have you judge me too harshly for some of the decisions I have made."

Sir John shook his head. "My dear girl, whatever your decisions, they have brought you to this place, and at the right time to save my life. How could I judge you harshly for those?"

"Still," I answered, "most times I do not think and act as other girls; you must remember that as I tell my tale."

Weed snorted his amusement at this. His father gave him a disapproving look. "Really Robert," he snapped, "you forget your manners as a gentleman to a lady."

"Mary is no lady," muttered Weed, avoiding his father's eye. "She dresses as a man."

"Silence, boy!" snapped Sir John.

"No, he is right," I said. "I am not typical of my sex, I know that. And I must now tell you how this came to be."

I rested my hands on my knees and looked across the clearing, thinking about where my story should start.

"I am the youngest stepchild of Sir Andrew Fox of Marchington Manor, in this county of Essex," I began. "I have three older brothers; Richard, the eldest, then Edward, then Henry. My true father died some six months before I was born, and my mother, Lady Eleanor Fox, married Sir Andrew before going into her confinement. But then she died in childbirth, and, I am sorry to say, Sir Andrew has never forgiven me for being the cause of the death of his new wife."

"But it was not your fault," Sir John said quickly.

"I know," I answered. "And in truth, he must know that also. But it is in his nature every day to take out his anger on me, and when I answer him back, to remind me that my coming into the world was the cause of her passing out of it."

Even Weed seemed shocked, in spite of himself. "That is unjust," he muttered.

"Perhaps, yes," I said. "But that is his nature."

"Not the nature of an honourable man, I warrant," observed Sir John. "But he married again, surely?" he asked. "What of your stepmother?"

"No, he did not marry again," I answered. "My mother was the only wife for him; he has remained unwed these seventeen years." I paused. "There have been many girls making the journey to his bedchamber, though none has, as yet, completed the journey to the altar."

"By Heaven!" exclaimed Sir John, "I am liking your stepfather less and less with each detail of him! So this is why you ran away this day?"

"No, my life was just tolerable until these few days past." I stared ahead, seeing not the clearing, but the many images of my daily life in Marchington Manor. "I was supposed to be the woman of the house from the age of eight, but I could not be, nor would not be, the picture of feminine charms that my father would have me be."

I thought a moment, looking for the right words to explain.

"My father worshipped my mother and made it clear every day that I was not fit to take her place. At the same time he would lavish praise on my brothers and give them all his care and attention. I came to believe that I had no value as a girl and should have been a boy like my brothers."

I turned to Sir John and held his eye. "I would have been as Richard, Edward and Henry – running free in the woods, fighting with wooden swords, shooting arrows – but this dismayed Sir Andrew greatly. He would have had me dressed in heavy, cumbersome gowns so I could not breathe; he would have had me sewing and serving foods to himself and my brothers. He would have crushed my spirit and it would not be crushed."

There was a silence while the two men absorbed this. I could read their thoughts as plain as if these were written in ink on their faces. They were considering how they would treat a daughter or sister acting in this way, and I could see it was not easy for them. Eventually Sir John shook his head as if to clear it, then he said, "And your brothers – how did they like this?"

"They mostly accepted me for what I was, as if I were a fourth. They taught me to ride and to fight with a sword."

"They taught you well," observed Sir John.

"You said that life was tolerable," said Weed slowly. "But how was it so if your father would have you acting like a… like a… proper…" he stumbled over the words, "like a proper girl, when you would act as a boy?"

"I would do as he wished on some occasions – at other times I would avoid his wrath by riding out in the forest or staying in my chambers."

Indeed, I would spend many an hour alone in my room; my only company being Rufus. He was a small bright-eyed robin who would come to my window looking for scraps of food, which I would willingly give him, in return for his undemanding companionship. He was certainly an excellent listener, never once interrupting my tales of hardship or my excitement if I had mastered a particularly difficult move with my sword.

"So what happened these few days past, that you must escape for good?" asked Sir John.

"It was when my stepfather said I must now marry and told me of the man he would have as my husband." I shuddered slightly; even the thought of that man upset me.

"But were you not betrothed as a child?" asked Weed. "That is normal for a girl of your birth."

"Yes," I answered. "I was originally betrothed to Francis de Courtney, the son of Sir Reginald de Courtney, when I was but six. It was meant as a strategic alliance between the Foxes and De Courtneys, in the face of some powerful families from Colchester. Francis was a nice lad and we met often as children, but I could see he was not interested in me as a future bride."

Weed raised his eyebrow in mute enquiry.

"I saw he was more interested in boys," I explained, quite matter-of-factly.

Sir John snorted with disapproval. "That is unnatural, and against the laws of the land. How could you know this?"

"As he grew into a man, he would comment on the looks of other boys, in a way I could see he felt for them as a man should feel for a woman. I challenged him on this one day and he admitted it was his secret."

"Were you not sickened by this?" asked Weed.

I shrugged. "Not particularly – as I say, he was a nice lad and we were friends. If I had married him, I have no doubt we would have lived a comfortable and understanding life. He at least would not have had me pretending to be a simpering girl – indeed, I think he liked me all the more for not wanting to wear gowns."

I chuckled as another memory came to mind. "On the day he told me, we passed a happy few hours comparing the relative merits of all the boys we knew. There were some we both liked, but he liked many more of them than I did."

"So why did you not marry him?" asked Sir John.

"A few weeks ago he caught a fever," I said. "We thought he would recover with ease, but it took a turn for the worse, went to his chest and he started to cough up blood. Within a couple of days, he was dead."

I felt sorry for Francis de Courtney and mourned his loss – he had truly been a friend.

"So who was the man chosen to replace him?" asked Sir John, bringing me back to the dreadful reality.

"It was Sir Reginald de Courtney, Francis's own father. He had been widowed a few years before and Sir Andrew decided it was the best way to continue with the alliance between our two families."

"And you do not care for him?"

Again I shuddered. "If my stepfather is a dominant bully, then Sir Reginald is ten times worse. Ten times ten, even." I looked up at them, each in turn. The horrified looks on their faces must have mirrored my own. "He is an old man, older than Sir Andrew. But if it were that only, I would most likely have accepted him." I shook my head. "No, it was his fierce temper and his stated belief that I am no better than a servant and a whore. And when we were alone, he told me that once we were married he would not tolerate me wearing any clothes but ornate gowns to please him, and that I would also exist only to serve his pleasure in the bed and in the house. I knew then that I had to get away from him, and from my own stepfather who would hand me over to him."

"So you saddled your horse and rode away?" asked Weed.

"Aye," I answered. "I did that this morning, while Sir Reginald and my stepfather went out hunting deer. I told my brothers I was riding over to the nearby town of Maldon to buy some sugar, but once I was on the road I turned the other way and headed west into the woods, whence I had travelled for a few hours. I was riding along the path when I saw you and the brigand." I smiled. "The rest you know."

There was a few moments' silence, as they absorbed my story. Then Sir John spoke. "So, we understand why you are as you are, Mary Fox," he said slowly. "I warrant any man would dismiss your concerns and tell you to act and dress as a proper woman and to become a dutiful wife. That is what is normal; what is expected."

I looked at him, fear turning in my belly. Now he had heard my story, it sounded as if maybe he did not believe in me. What if he tried to take me back to Marchington Manor and Sir Reginald? I looked at where Hestia stood patiently across the clearing, quickly measuring the distance with my eye, working out how fast I could get up, run to her, mount up and be away. Then he spoke again.

"But I am not any man," he said. "I am a man whose life has been saved by your actions, and I have given my word not to take you back."

My belly stopped turning and I let out the breath I must have been holding.

"So again, we agree to journey together back to Nacton," he said. "I will offer you my protection, if you will help me bring the Broken Sword back home – and so lift the curse on my lands and my family."

Just then we heard a faint shout in the distance and the thud of horses' hooves.

For a moment we were frozen, then we quickly stood up, listening intently.

"Riders coming," said Sir John, looking east. "Most likely some travellers on their way to London."

Then we heard the baying of dogs.

"It is a hunt," said Weed.

There was another shout. It sounded like, "They have the scent! The dogs have her trail!"

My blood froze to ice in my veins. It was a voice I recognised.

It was Sir Reginald de Courtney.

"Oh yes, for sure it is a hunt," I whispered. "It is the one that set off this morning from Marchington Manor to chase deer."

I looked at them both in horror.

"But now they are hunting me!"

4

CHAPTER FOUR

For a brief moment the three of us stood in shocked silence, as the enormity of the danger sank in.

Then suddenly all was action. Weed and Sir John ran to their horses, and I was about to do the same, when an idea came to me. Instead, I ran to the brigand's cart.

"What would you do?" shouted Sir John over his shoulder. "It will slow us up – we must abandon it!"

I reached the cart and opened the hatch at the back, then ripped off both my sleeves, tearing at the stitching with such force that they came easily apart from the rest of my chemise at the shoulder. I threw them in. "This will slow the hunt up, not us!" I shouted, then rammed the latch down as hard as I could and ran over to Hestia. She was skitting about, her eyes wide and anxious at the sound of yelping dogs approaching; as I put my foot in the stirrup she was already starting to move at pace and I had to use all my strength to run alongside then pull myself up into the saddle.

Sir John wheeled his mount round behind me and we followed Weed out of the clearing. "You plan to distract the dogs with your sleeves?" he shouted over to me.

"Yes!" I yelled back over my shoulder. "My stepfather will have taught them to hunt my scent. My sleeves will make them think I am hiding in there – it may give us some time!"

"Good thinking, my child!" he answered, as we urged our horses out of the clearing and onto the forest path.

Our way was relatively clear and we made fast progress, soon reaching a large oak tree where the path split into two. Weed swung left but Hestia shied to the right. At the last moment I managed to pull her to the left, and was able to follow Weed's direction. I trusted he knew where he was going, although any path would be good if it allowed us to escape the hunt. The new one was also wide and easy to ride through; Hestia picked her way quickly over the low roots and around the small trees that appeared. I was pleased that I was able to keep pace with Weed's mount ahead.

As we thundered through the forest, I imagined Sir Reginald and Sir Andrew entering the clearing to find the dogs baying at the brigand's cart, scratching at the latch in their desperation to get inside, believing me to be hidden in its darkness. I imagined the hunters pushing at the small latch with their fingers to open it, but having to lever it up with a sword as I had jammed it down so tightly. I could see the look of disappointment on their faces as the door opened and revealed nothing more than an empty cart and a pair of my sleeves. I particularly saw the anger on my stepfather's face as he realised his daughter had tricked him. I smiled to myself as my horse flew out over a small ditch crossing our path.

But then my smile froze on my face.

What sort of man – what sort of evil man – was my stepfather, that would hunt a child of his family as one would hunt an innocent deer? What sort of man would capture this child and hand her over to a sick monster of a husband, some years his elder; a husband who would use her as an idle plaything and deliberately upset her for his own amusement? And what sort of a society must we live in, where a man can do this to his daughter, and have the full blessing of the law in so doing?

I decided, as I galloped through the forest that day, that such servitude would never be for me. I decided that I, Mary Fox, was better than that – and if the laws meant a man could do such things, then they were bad laws. I decided that I would do all in my power to live my own life – not the one chosen for me by a man.

As I thought this, I noticed Weed's horse had to jump an unusually high root, and almost immediately, I jumped it also. After that there were more roots to jump, as well as a fallen log. Then the path narrowed and many low branches appeared, that must be ducked under.

With such a narrow, overgrown path, it was no longer possible to fly along at such breakneck speed, and Weed slowed down to a trot. As I also slowed, I turned to look behind me for Sir John.

But the path behind me was quite empty.

My stomach lurched and I thought I would be sick.

"Robert!" I called, and he turned on his horse to look back. "Your father! Sir John! He is not with us!"

Weed brought his horse to a stop and wheeled it round to face me. "By the risen Christ!" he gasped. "Where is he?"

"Belike he went right at the oak tree when we went left," I said. "My horse shied right, and he was just behind me. He may have gone that way and not been able to stop." I paused, considering. "It is a different path, but it does not mean he is necessarily captured." I fear I was trying to convince myself more than Weed, and his next words sent my spirits to my boots.

"Nay, that is the path to the river. He would be trapped at its edge…" he tailed off, his face visibly paling. "Then he is captured, for sure."

I listened intently. There was no sound of horses, men or dogs on our trail – which could be because they were stopped by the river with Sir John.

I took a breath and held his eye.

"We will have to go back, and quietly," I said, sounding more resolved than I was actually feeling. He opened his mouth, then appeared to think better and closed it. I wondered if he was going to suggest we abandon Sir John and go on? Once again I questioned what it was with this man that he would abandon such a kind-hearted father to his fate, and resolved to keep up my guard with great care.

"We will tether our horses here and go back on foot," I said. "We can be quieter that way." He gave no objection and slipped from the saddle. I did likewise. Then we tied the horses to a small tree and started back down the path.

It was difficult going on foot, with roots and logs in our path that would be but a small hop for a horse, while we must spring to the top and leap athletically down. I thanked God that I had the foresight to be clothed as a boy – to attempt such feats in a gown did not bear contemplation. Weed kept pace behind me; I could hear him huffing and puffing as he leapt from each obstacle.

After some time we arrived back at the oak tree and paused a moment to catch our breath.

"Do you hear anything?" he whispered.

I refrained from pointing out that he also possessed a pair of ears, but instead I slowed my breath so I could hear better. There was no sound, save the birds singing in their joyful ignorance of our situation, and the wind rustling through the trees with the same carefree indifference. "No," I said. "They must have stopped. We must proceed now in total silence."

Cautiously we turned onto the other path. I glanced back at Weed. Once again his green clothing provided some measure of camouflage in the forest. I glanced down at my own white chemise and pale bare arms – I might as well have blown a horn to announce my arrival. Quickly I reached down and scooped a handful of earth from the forest floor, then rubbed it over my arms and chemise, till they were brown in colour and mottled in appearance. I then did the same with my face. Weed saw what I was doing and he also scooped up earth for his face. I nodded approval then waved us quietly forward.

The path to the river was broad and clear, so I kept us a few yards inside the trees for better cover. This slowed our progress considerably, but I did not want to risk being seen. At one point we had no option but to step out onto the path as our way was blocked by a mighty fallen tree trunk, but fortunately there was no triumphant shout and we had not been seen.

A few minutes later, Weed whispered, "If I recall, the river is round the next bend." Immediately I stopped and listened carefully.

The muffled sound of men's voices could now be heard.

I recognised the harsh tones of my stepfather's voice, and of Sir Reginald.

Then I recognised the voice of Sir John.

I turned to see if Weed had heard the same, and he nodded at me with wild white eyes.

We needed to see and hear clearly what was happening. I licked my finger and held it up to test the direction of the wind, then silently waved Weed forward. We crept as quietly as we could through the trees, keeping upwind of the river.

A shimmering, dappled light appeared in the distance, which I soon made out to be the water. The voices sounded again, very close. I signalled Weed to take cover behind a convenient tree, while I hid behind the one next to it.

I peered out at a scene from my worst nightmare.

Sir John was facing away from us with his back to a slim tree, his hands tied together behind it. My stepfather and Sir Reginald were facing him side by side, with the dogs held firmly by two huntsmen. As we were upwind, the dogs made no recognition of our presence.

Sir Reginald was smiling coldly as he held the Broken Sword; turning it in his hand so that the golden light flashed around the forest.

"I have already told you," said Sir John, with weary droop to his shoulders, "it is of no value; a mere trinket."

"Yet your gaze never leaves it as it moves," observed Sir Reginald slowly, his own eyes narrowing. "I wager it is of immense value to you." He turned and threw it to my stepfather. "What say you, Andrew?"

My stepfather caught it deftly and turned it around, studying it. "I would say it is indeed of high value, Reginald." He picked at one of the emeralds, as if trying to extract it from its mount. "These stones alone are worth a king's ransom. It could be broken up for the stones – and for the gold."

Sir John must have flinched at this. Sir Reginald looked at him with a nasty smile. "Aye, I thought as much," he said. "This piece is most assuredly worth a king's ransom to you – that you are sickened by the thought of its destruction."

He tapped his hand on the hilt of his own sword, his thin face deep in thought. "A ransom, eh? Aye, that's what we will do. We will hold you and this hilt as hostage, against the return home of the woman you have taken from us – the headstrong Mary Fox."

"I warrant she is already in the next county," said Sir John, defiance in his voice. "She will not know that you have me."

"Oh, I doubt that," interjected my stepfather. "As like as not she is watching us even now." He looked across the forest. Weed and I ducked quickly out of sight behind our trees, my blood hammering loudly in my ears. "As you may have noticed, my dear Sir John, this daughter of mine fancies herself as some kind of adventurer in boy's clothing. I'faith," he continued, "it is most unnatural and quite un-womanly –

but she needs must act this part and like as not she has tracked us here." There was a silence, and I pictured his gaze raking across the foliage, looking for some small sign of our presence. I shrank further behind my tree.

"Are you here, my dearly beloved daughter?" he shouted. "Are you watching us even now?"

I think in truth he fancied he had spotted us, and was now playing a game.

"If you are here, come out and we can discuss this like civilized people!" Again he paused. "God damn you, girl! I am your father! Get out here now or the consequences will be the worse for you, and for this man!"

I shot a look at Weed and put a warning finger to my lips. He nodded his head briefly, to make it clear he would stay silent and do nothing to give us away – but I could not help but feel he was more in fear for himself than for his father.

"Very well. If you are here, my child," Sir Andrew continued, "let me tell you what happens next." His voice dropped slightly. "Sir Reginald and I will take this man – this man that you seem to have formed a bond with, in but a few hours – and we will hold him hostage at Marchington. If you want to have him released, you will return home, dress as befits your sex and be married forthwith to Sir Reginald. Once you have made your vows before God, then Sir John, his son and this broken relic of a hilt, will be free to go."

"And if she does not come?" This was Sir Reginald.

"Then we will have no use for this wandering knight," said my stepfather slowly. "I give her three days – then he will be..." he paused and I waited for the inevitable. "He will be... disposed of."

I heard Sir Reginald laugh and my stepfather raised his voice again. "Do you hear me, Mary Fox, my sometime daughter? Do you hear me? Come home openly as a penitent daughter within three days, or you will have this man's death as a burden on your soul for all eternity."

I felt physically sick. How cursed was I to have such an evil, godless man as a stepfather?

"I understand you saved this man's life this morning, Mary!" he continued. "It seems you must do so once again!"

"You would be an adventurer, Mary!" called Sir Reginald. "But I would have you as an obedient wife! Come home and submit to your duty!"

Again I looked across at Weed – but this time he did not turn his head or meet my gaze.

"Untie the man from the tree," said my stepfather "and secure the rope to my horse's saddle. He can run behind us back to Marchington."

There were sounds of scuffles as Sir John was transferred, then the sound of the horses trotting off and the dogs yelping as they ran as well. I shuddered as I pictured Sir John forced to run behind Sir Andrew's horse, struggling to avoid falling to the forest floor and being flayed by the roots and stones.

"Three days, Mary!" came my stepfather's voice as they trotted away. "Three days!"

The hoof beats and yelps faded into the distance.

Silence descended on the forest.

I let out a long, deep breath, forcing my heart to slow to its normal pace.

"So what would you do, then?" This was Weed, leaning against his tree, observing me with an almost casual interest.

"What would I do? What would I do?" I found my voice rising. "By the Lord's wounds, it is not my problem! It is your father they hold hostage is it not? It is your mother and sister's health that is secured by the return of the precious Broken Sword!" I shook my head. "Did you not hear that odious Sir Reginald demand that I return to marry him? Believe me, I have more reason to head away from Marchington than to head back." I strode over to him, now finding it difficult to control my rising temper. "Whereas you, Wee... Master Robert, you who should be in great haste to rescue your father, you seem quite indifferent to his fate!" I stopped in front of him. "Aye, it is of a piece with your action this morning, when you abandoned him to the brigand!"

He said nothing, but started to breathe in rapid, short breaths, his thin face starting to turn bright red like a crushed strawberry.

"Why is that?" I demanded. "Why did you prepare to abandon him this morning and again now? I have to know."

I stepped back and waited. Eventually his breathing returned to normal and he looked up at me.

"You should know," he said. "You have no love for your father. I too have no love for mine."

This did not make sense. "But your father is a good and honourable man. He is everything a father should be, while mine is a beast," I said. "What has he done to you, that you must hate him so?"

He took a deep breath, considering me. "I will tell you," he said. "Then you can be a truer judge of my actions."

He slowly got up.

"I will tell you. Then we can decide what is best to do."

5

CHAPTER FIVE

"You are correct when you say my father is a good and honourable man," Weed began, as we made our way back along the forest path towards the place where we had tethered the horses. "He is indeed honourable and upright – he is truer than the flight of an arrow. In all Suffolk, he is known as a man who will stand by his friends and cast down his enemies." He stepped carefully over a log. "And in truth, he has precious few of those."

"He seems to be the very model of virtue," I agreed, and Weed nodded in return. "Then why must you hate him so?" I asked once again.

He stopped with his foot on another log and looked back at me, his eyes moving anxiously across my face. "You have grown up with a stepfather you knew to be a monster – who blamed you for the death of your mother and used you most harshly." he said.

"Yes," I agreed. "But yours is not…"

"No, yet every person I have ever met since I was a boy has told me time and again what a good man he is. What a great man." He regarded me with big eyes. "Every person, from my mother and sister to the tenants on our land, has remarked on this – and each has told me that as his only son, I needs must live up to this ideal standard of manhood." There was a slight catch in his voice and I thought perhaps a small tear had appeared in the corner of his eye. "I have been measured continually to perfection, and God knows, I have every time failed to measure up." He sniffed and the tear started to roll down his cheek towards his wispy ginger beard. "Do you know, Christ himself could not measure up! So what chance do I have – I, a youth who cannot fight with a sword, who runs away from danger? I, who mostly sees the bad in others, when my father will always see the good alone?"

Oh, I would have laughed if it were not so sad – and if laughing would not have destroyed what small, fragile self-belief he might still have possessed.

I considered my response carefully.

"There is good in you, Master Robert, I'll warrant. Good indeed." He still had one shoe on the log, so I gestured towards it. "Sit, and we will take stock."

He sat, and as I sat next to him on the soft, mossy log, another tear started its journey down his cheek. I could see I would have to tread carefully if I were to help him find his self-belief – and he would have to be strong if we were to save Sir John and his womenfolk. Yes – and save them we must. I could see, with absolute certainty, that Sir John must be saved and the Broken Sword returned to Nacton – and I could not do it alone. So I considered my next words with great care.

"If I would be the girl my stepfather would have me be, then would I be true to myself?" He gazed tearfully at me and shook his head. "Indeed," I continued, "I would be lying to myself and so to God." He gave a hesitant nod. "And, if you would be but a mirror of your father, would that make you true to yourself?" He shook his head again, which caused further tears to spill down his cheek. I pressed on. "No, you would also be lying to yourself and to God." He nodded. I took a breath. "And if you were not lying to yourself or to God, Master Robert…" I placed my hand gently on his leg, to signify that we had reached the kernel of his problem. "What would your true self be?"

He did not answer immediately; seeking inspiration instead in the high trees and in the crows that flew and cawed in circles above them.

I waited while he considered his reply, careful not to place him under too much pressure.

After a while he turned to me and said carefully, "Mary, if you must ask, then in truth, this is what I would be. I would be a fine gentleman, possessed of a good wife and many children." He paused and swallowed twice. "I would enjoy a comfortable life in my manor house in Suffolk." He nodded to himself as he stared across the forest – seeing not the trees and birds, I fancy, but instead his ideal existence. "I would not need a sword or to go out to war – nay, I would husband the fields and the tenants, and I would be a fine landowner, who grows fat and content with his family around him." He fixed me with watery eyes. "As you ask, Mary Fox, that is what my true self would be."

"And it can be," I said, giving his leg a small squeeze.

He was silent a while.

"Then what must we do?"

I had been giving this much thought since my step-father's challenge back by the river, and the seed of an idea was beginning to form in my mind. But it would need more consideration, as well as clear instruction to Weed on the part he would need to play, plus preparation in clothing and appearance. And it would carry the highest risk. We would not get a second chance.

"I am thinking through my plan," I said. "And I will tell you your part when I have all the pieces in place." He smiled weakly – causing me to wonder if I had yet done enough to build his confidence. I would have to keep reinforcing it so he could perform the role I had in mind. Once again, I resolved to be more encouraging; now I understood why he felt as he did towards his father, I could be more supportive.

He sniffed and wiped his nose on his sleeve.

He was still 'Weed'. That had not changed.

I smiled at him. "Then let us get back to our horses and find an inn for the night." I stood up. "Come on, we have much to do if we are to rescue your father and your family."

I set off through the forest with him following. We walked in silence along the path, each lost in our own thoughts until we reached the horses, which thankfully had not untethered themselves or strayed. I hoped Weed's thoughts on this brief walk had been positive and self-affirming. I knew that I had started the process of healing his soul, but I was realistic enough to know the job was far from complete.

As we mounted up, I said, "We will stay tonight in the Blue Boar in Maldon – it is a good inn and I know the innkeeper there – he is a friend who will not betray us to my stepfather or Sir Reginald de Courtney. Then we must plan and prepare our rescue mission on Marchington Manor.

Weed did not answer, so I wheeled my horse round and fixed him with my most steady stare. "Are you with me, Master Robert?"

He had his head down, and I thought he had lost any new-found confidence. I felt sure he would now deny me.

"Are you with me, Master Robert?" I repeated more strongly, my heart in my mouth.

He looked up, and I was relieved to see some resolve come into the way he lifted his chin. "Aye, Mary Fox," he said in a small voice. "I am."

"Good." I wheeled Hestia back round, facing down the path from the forest. "Then let us make our plans and get your father and the Broken Sword out of Marchington Manor."

"Aye," he said behind me, this time in a stronger voice.

I looked back. "It will carry risk," I said, wanting to test his resolve.

"Aye, it will," he answered, his voice stronger still, and even a little lower pitched.

I turned back to cover my smile. "Then let us make haste for Maldon," I said. With that I dug my heels into the sides of my horse and set off at a fast canter without looking behind me again.

---O---

We spent the next two days at the Blue Boar in Maldon, making our plans and securing the clothing and equipment necessary for our foray to Marchington Manor.

I also spent much time continuing to work on Weed himself, wanting to do all I could to build on my success in the forest and help him become his own man.

It was not easy work, and once or twice I felt close to abandoning the task, but despite the setbacks I began to believe that we were making progress.

It was the second evening. We were sitting by the fire in the parlour of the Blue Boar, our tankards of ale in front of us, as we went over the plan for the third time.

"And you are sure you can keep up this pretence?" I asked, after I had set out his role and he had once again descended into tears. Controlling my temper, I said, "I need you to be strong. I need you to play this part well." Then I decided to be harsh to be kind. "Or in truth, Master Robert, you will never grow old and fat with your family in days to come."

It seemed to be the kick in the behind that he needed. "Aye," he answered hesitantly.

"You must be certain," I said, pressing my advantage.

"Aye," he said again, this time with greater resolve.

"Excellent," I answered. "Then tell me again what you must do."

He repeated his part in the plan as we had agreed it, and although I had to resolve some small details, in essence now he had it correct.

"Good," I said. "We go tonight – in the darkest hour before dawn."

6

CHAPTER SIX

Our horses made no sound as we rode towards March-ington Manor in the darkness. I had made Weed wrap rags about his horse's hooves to mask the noise and I had done the same myself; I wanted to ensure we did not alert any resident or guard until we were ready to do so ourselves. I also led a spare horse by the reins, saddled and ready for Sir John to make good his escape. It had cost me a pretty sum of coin, but it was worth it to ensure we three could get away with speed.

The night was cold as we trod the path out of Maldon; matching the chill in my heart as we set out towards the building that I had once called home. I had vowed only a few days before that I would never return; yet here I was, once again riding the familiar path back. The trees that I knew so well in the daylight loomed over us like menacing giants in the dark.

We turned a corner and I hissed a command to Weed to stop. Before us were the high gates of Marchington Manor; my stepfather's golden crest visible as only a black shape against the night sky.

"We tether the horses just up ahead," I whispered.

"As you say," Weed whispered back, although his voice was too soft. Too hesitant.

I glanced behind; he was but a dark shape and I could not determine the set of his face. Certainly the tone of his voice gave me cause for some concern; I could not have him fail on me now.

"Courage, Master Robert," I said, in a determined manner. "You have the plan and your part well learned."

"Aye," he answered. "But now the time has come, my resolve is weakened."

"You can do it." I nodded to reassure him, although I warrant he could not see the gesture. "The fat, contented Sir Robert Fitzwilliam and his family yet to come – they will thank you for your actions this night."

There was a long silence. I began to think that I should change the plan and have him stay here while I attempted the rescue alone, but then he said, "I will make the attempt, Mary. I will do it. For my family now and for the family yet to come."

"Good." I fear I could not disguise the relief in my voice. "Then we must tether the horses up ahead. Let us go."

We walked the horses forward a few quiet yards, until I could make out the familiar shape of an old oak tree a few feet back from the wall. I leapt lightly from Hestia's saddle and heard Weed dismount also, then I took all three reins and tied them securely around a low branch. The horses were out of sight, but close enough to the gate for our escape once we had Sir John. I prayed that they would stay silent.

"Come," I hissed again, then made my way back towards the main gates. "Are you ready to play your part?"

This time there was less hesitation. "Yes."

"Good." I crouched low into the bushes beside the brick pillar. "Then go to it."

I could just see him pull the hood of his cloak up over his head, then step out in front of the gate. He took out a stick and gave a couple of taps on the metal posts. This produced a sound like the tolling of a bell, sounding unnaturally loud in the still of the night.

For a minute or two there was no movement from beyond the gate, then I heard some footsteps on the path and a man appeared. I could just make out the shape of a halberd in his hand and a metal helmet on his head.

"Who goes there?" His voice was sleepy, but I recognised it as Tom Reeves, one of my stepfather's older liverymen, and I breathed a sigh of relief. My plan had depended on it being Tom on guard this night.

Weed spoke in the guttural, old man's voice, that I had made him practice for many hours. "I am a traveller from Suffolk, on my way to London. I have been on the road these two days and I needs must eat. I ask only some ale and bread, good sir."

"I must not let anyone in during the night, lest they be up to no good. Strict orders." Tom's voice was now less sleepy – more alert.

Weed played his part well. "I am not up to no good, I assure you, sir."

"But I have my orders. Good night to you." There was the sound of a foot turning on the gravel path and steps going away.

"Wait!" Weed called. The footsteps stopped.

We had thought this would happen, so had prepared a further plan. "I have some rum here in my bag," Weed said quickly. "Is that not a fair trade for some bread and ale?

The footsteps came closer again.

"Some rum for bread and ale?"

"Yes."

There was a pause. I held my breath.

"Wait here." The footsteps crunched away down the path.

I breathed out in relief and stood up. I went over to Weed. "Well done, sir," I whispered. "Your part was played to perfection."

"Thus far."

"Yes, but thus far, it is going well. Now," I said, "as I hoped, this guard is indeed the old soldier, Tom Reeves. He will do anything for a nip of rum. Play your part well in the coming few minutes and you will get his confidence."

I sank back into the bushes and we waited until Tom returned, a burning torch casting red light and long shadows across his face and all around him. He stopped by the gate, but made no move to open it. "I have a bag here with some bread and a costrel of ale," he said, holding it up in his free hand. "Pass through the rum and I will make fair exchange."

"Come closer," croaked Weed. "I would see what you have."

Tom came right up to the gate and took what looked like a small loaf of rye bread out of his bag, "Here – is this enough to satisfy you? Now pass me the rum."

"Tom?" croaked Weed instead, his voice rising to show excitement. "Tom Reeves? I am sure I recognise your voice."

"Aye," said Tom suspiciously. "I am he. Who asks?"

"Rob Godfrey! Have you forgot? We were together at the Siege of Boulogne!"

"I was there, but I do not recall a Rob Godfrey," answered Tom suspiciously.

"I was under the command of Sergeant Ginter."

"Sergeant Ginter? I too was under Ginter!" Now Tom was hooked, just like a pike in a stream. His next words confirmed our success. "For sure, I have forgot you, but we must have known each other. In truth, it was many years ago. Forgive me, I am sure we were close; it is just I had forgot…" I smiled to myself in the dark. If the lie is brazen enough, it will be believed.

"You must come in; we will share the rum and relive the siege together!" Tom reached for the keys at his belt, selected one and unlocked the gate. "Come through!"

"With pleasure," Weed answered. As Tom pulled the gate open, Weed walked forward, then suddenly he stopped. "My eyes are not what they once were," he muttered. "Can you light the path for me with your flame?"

"Surely." Tom turned round and held his brazier out over the path.

I slipped silently through the gate behind them and sank into the shadows on the far side.

Weed continued through. "Thank you, Tom," he said, as

the other man closed the gate then locked it. "Most kind of you."

I grinned to myself in the dark, as I crouched beside the wall.

Thus far my plan had worked, and Weed had played his part well.

I held my breath as they walked away down the path together, conversing quietly. Again, I smiled to myself. Tom always had a loose tongue about his Boulogne exploits, and I had passed many an hour in his ramshackle watchman's hut listening to his tales. I certainly had plenty of material to teach Weed all he needed to play the part of the old soldier; it had remained only to blacken his face with soot and grey his hair with chalk, and we had the perfect transformation. I prayed that the rum – which Weed would only pretend to drink – would dull Tom's wits sufficiently for us to make good our escape, once I had located Sir John and the Broken Sword.

But this would be no easy task.

As I made my way silently towards the house under the cover of the darkness, I knew my planning and preparation would only take me so far; I would also need a goodly slice of luck if I was to succeed in my venture. Indeed, as I came to the edge of the lawns and observed the monstrous black shape of Marchington Manor against the night sky, I felt my nerve starting to fail me. What if Sir Andrew had kept awake in the night and was waiting for me inside the house? What if he had put his dogs on guard outside the cellar where I believed Sir John would be held prisoner? How could I think that I, a girl of but seventeen years, could possibly succeed in such a daring rescue?

Such doubts and fears played deeply on my mind, and I wondered for a moment if I should somehow get back out of the gate, leap upon dear Hestia's back and continue alone on the journey had I begun three days before.

But then I thought of poor Sir John held against his will facing almost certain death; the Broken Sword out of its rightful place, putting Lady Anne Fitzwilliam and her daughter Margaret in such anguish; and even poor Weed, prepared to risk his life playing the part of an old soldier in order to help free the father he could not live up to... and I stiffened my resolve, took a deep breath to calm my racing heart and continued to tread stealthily towards the house.

I made my way round to the back, keeping at first to the grass where I knew my feet would make no noise. Then I came to the edge, and looked at the treacherous gravel path that circled the house – a path I would need to cross to get to the kitchen door.

Normally it would not be possible to cross such a path in the still of the night without making a noise that would seem like a hundred marching men – but I had thought of this and carried in the pack on my back two thick rolls of blanket kindly loaned by the innkeeper at the Blue Boar. I carefully laid out the first roll at the edge of the path and stepped lightly onto it. My plan worked – there was no noise. I walked softly to the end and took the other roll from my pack, then laid it beyond the first. Stepping onto this second blanket, I collected the first then walked across. I repeated the manoeuvre a few more times until I had silently crossed the width of the path.

Arriving at the kitchen door, I was feeling breathlessly

elated at conquering this last challenge, but I knew there were many more to come. I placed my two rolls of blanket in the shadows, then took a moment in front of the door to try and get my breathing down to a more normal level. Once it was calmer, I addressed the door itself. It was locked, as I knew it would be, but I also knew that if one took a stout stick and pushed it into the space between the door and the frame just by the lock, then the old, worn bolt could easily be levered clear and the door opened. I had come and gone from the house this way many a time, when my stepfather had foolishly believed he had me secure.

Taking the stick I had brought from my pack, I pushed it hard into the space then pulled it to the side, and was rewarded with the door swinging open.

There was a loud creak as it moved. With a muttered curse I stopped it immediately and stood still, waiting to hear if the alarm was raised inside the house.

Why had it creaked? It had always swung silently before. Then I remembered there had been heavy rains a few days earlier – perhaps there was new rust inside the hinges. Thankfully there were no shouts from inside. Fearing to open the door further in case it creaked again, I eased myself through the narrow space, then stepped into the kitchen.

The embers of the fire lit the room in an eerie orange glow. I could see some servants asleep on truckle beds in the corner, although I knew from my earlier comings and goings that they slept like the dead – the cook and steward were fearsome fellows who worked them hard. I crept as quietly as I could across the flagstone floor, past the dry hearth for roasting boar and venison, the wet hearth for soups and pottage, the meat table where the joints were prepared and the sugar table where the puddings and sweet fancies were made, then out of the kitchens and into the pitch-black corridor towards the wine cellar.

Had I guessed correctly where my stepfather would have put Sir John? The small lockable office room in the corner of the cellars was the most secure room in the house – he had to be keeping Sir John in there.

The cellars were low vaulted brick rooms opening off a central corridor, which was accessed down some steps at the far end of the long passageway from the kitchens. I felt my way in the dark to the top of the steps and stopped, stilling my breath and straining to hear any sounds from the corridor below.

In particular, I was listening for the sound of dogs.

In sick dread I realised the sound I could faintly hear from the bottom of the stairs was the breathing and little soft whines that my stepfather's two wolfhounds, Sirius and Janus, were used to making in their sleep. Despite my dread I permitted myself some small satisfaction – if the dogs were on guard, then I had guessed correctly where Sir John was being held.

But my satisfaction must be short-lived – if I could not get them quietly out of the way, how could Sir John possibly be rescued?

I took off my pack and sat in the dark with my back to the cold stone wall as I considered this seemingly impossible task. Any attempt to get past the dogs would awaken them. At best they would bark like devils and alert the whole household. At worst they would bark just as loudly, while also attacking me with their fearsome teeth. No doubt my stepfather had kept them starved of meat so they would more likely attack any would-be rescuer...

Meat... now there was a thought...

There would be bones, offcuts and waste meat in the kitchens – it was kept in an old barrel for boiling down to make broth. If I were lucky there may just be some meat I could use to tempt two starving dogs from their sentry-post.

I hefted my pack onto my shoulder and crept quietly back along the length of the passage towards the orange light of the kitchens. In the dull glow I could see the barrel, standing beside the preparation table. I padded softly over to it and peered inside. It was hard to see its contents as the shadows were deep, so I put my hand gingerly inside, and rummaged in the disgusting mess. After a moment I felt a slime-covered bone, which I took out and examined. It still had some small amount of meat and sinew on it and smelled quite rank, but I felt sure it would appeal to the dogs – for all that it turned my stomach – and its strong odour would mask my own scent. I put it on the floor while I rummaged further in the barrel, and produced a second bone, much like the first. Then I rummaged one final time, and triumphantly pulled out a small fatty offcut.

Holding the meat and bones carefully, I once again stepped into the pitch blackness of the passageway and felt my way slowly back to the top of the cellar stairs.

When I had located them, I put the meat offcut down at the top, then made my way round to the far side. There was a door at the end of the corridor which led to some storerooms, so I felt my way over and opened it, then stood behind it and waited.

After a few moments I heard the sound of claws on the stairs, as the dogs – no doubt woken from their slumbers by the pungent aroma of the offcut – made their way up. Then I heard the sound of eating. When that was finished, I turned and tossed the two bones through the door behind me. The noise alerted them and I heard them run past, chasing the sound and smell. I thanked God that they had not chosen to bark at the same time, as I closed and latched the door behind them, securing them in the storerooms to chew contentedly – and quietly – on the bones.

I felt my way back to the stairs and went cautiously down, tapping my toe on each step until I came to the flagstones of the cellar corridor. Then I moved along the corridor until I came to the little office room at the end.

I knocked gently on the old oak door and put my mouth to the lock plate.

"Sir John?" I whispered.

There was no answer. I tapped again, and this time my heart leapt as I heard the sound of movement inside.

"Who's there?" came a soft voice from the other side of the lock.

"Is that Sir John?" I asked breathlessly. I thought I recognised his voice, but I needed to be sure.

"Aye." He paused. "Mary? Mary Fox? Is that you?"

"Yes," I answered. "Yes it is."

"God's Wounds, woman, what are you doing here at this time?"

He must have been still half-asleep; not thinking clearly.

"I am here to rescue you," I said, with more confidence than I felt. "I've come to get you out."

7

CHAPTER SEVEN

I felt by the door for the key that usually hung there, and by God's good grace it was in its place. I unlocked the door and pulled it slowly open. There was a patting and rustling sound, as if Sir John were feeling his way slowly along the wall towards me, then I felt his hand find mine. I pulled him out of the room.

"By Heaven, Mary Fox," he whispered, close to my ear. "You do not rest in your endeavours, do you?"

"I could not let them murder you," I muttered.

"So you knew that was their plan?" He gave a low chuckle, but without mirth. "Then you were there in the forest when your father and that dreadful Sir Reginald took me?"

My heart leapt at the sound of another person saying out loud that Sir Reginald was indeed a dreadful man. I took a breath and said, "Yes. Robert and I tracked back and came to the clearing. We were concealed behind trees and we heard all that passed."

"Aye – and your father's challenge."

"I could not risk that he would kill you. I had to come."

"He near killed me that very day by dragging me behind his horse." His hand tightened on mine, no doubt at the memory. "Not only were my arms all but pulled from my shoulders, but it was as much as I could do not to fall over and be flayed to death. Fortunately I managed to keep up with his pace for the whole time. It was but a trot, not a canter."

"He obviously decided to keep you alive."

"Indeed, and I very much intend to stay that way," he said. "So, what is your plan? I warrant that you have one?"

"Of a sort," I said. "Robert is distracting the guard and I have a third horse tethered nearby. We must make our way to the gate as quiet as mice."

"There are dogs in the corridor."

"Aye, but just now they are occupied with bones to chew, behind a closed door. Our way is clear."

There was a silence, then he said carefully, "Ever resourceful, Mistress Mary. I should not have doubted you."

"It was but one challenge and we have many more yet," I said. "Come. We must away to the horses."

I made to pull him towards the corridor, but felt him resist.

"Come!" I repeated. "We must be away before the dogs bark to be released."

"Wait!" he hissed. "The Broken Sword! We have to get it first."

"The Broken Sword? Do you not have it with you?"

"It was taken from me by your father."

"He took it from you?" I repeated, realising I sounded like the village fool.

"Aye."

I stamped my foot with annoyance. "I should have known he would do that. It is his style." In my mind I could see the smile on my stepfather's face as he took the sword from Sir John. He would have studied it with a show of care, before no doubt handing it casually to a servant to take away. In truth he knew how precious it was – so he would have been deliberately dismissive of it, just for devilment.

Sir John let my hand drop. "He said something I could not fathom when he took it."

"What was that?"

"He said it was 'his most effective alarm' if you came for me."

"An 'alarm' – why would he say that?"

Now I was thinking fast. So my stepfather knew that I would come, not in the open as a penitent daughter, but in the night as a rescuer. He then knew I could free Sir John with ease – but he was not concerned because I would have to come after the precious Broken Sword. So he could sleep content, safe in the knowledge that even if I got this far unchallenged, he would capture me when I came for the Broken Sword, because it was his 'alarm'. What did he mean by that? It could only mean that it was placed somewhere that could not be retrieved without somehow awakening the house. Where could that be...? Somewhere that made a loud noise... My mind went back to the door to the kitchens that creaked unexpectedly when I opened it... But that was too unusual – I did not think it was part of his plan... Where else was guaranteed to make a loud noise and could conceal the Broken Sword – and would be a place I would know well…?

I would know well…!

I gave a short, triumphant laugh.

"What is it?" asked Sir John out of the pitch blackness.

"I know where he has hidden it," I said. "And he is right – it will raise an alarm – a most effective one. Retrieving it will make a noise to waken the whole house.

"By Heaven, he is a cruel joker, your father," muttered Sir John. "Where is it?"

"A place where the joke is on us," I said flatly. "It is down the disused well at the back of the house, most probably in the bucket. The capstan is old and broken; not only does it creak, but it makes a noise like a sword crashing onto a shield each time the handle is turned. Raising it in the still of the night it would make a racket fit to waken the dead."

There was a silence as Sir John thought this through. "But can you not just lean over and pull the rope up without the using the capstan?" he asked eventually. "That would avoid it making a noise."

"You could try," I answered, "but the bucket might sway and hit the side of the well, making a noise in itself."

I thought of how my stepfather's devious mind worked. He would want to be certain we had no other options, so how would he maximise the risk for us…?

Suddenly I saw with total clarity what he had done – as if a curtain had been pulled back to reveal his dreadful scheme in full. I had to admire his cunning – it was simple and most effective.

"No," I said grimly. "He has tried to give us no option but

to turn the capstan. I'll warrant that the Broken Sword will have been hooked just over the edge of the bucket, so that if the bucket sways and hits hard on the side of the well, it will fall off and be lost forever in the depths." I shook my head in the darkness. "No, he knows the only way we can get it back safe is to slowly turn the capstan and lift it up on the rope – and to raise the alarm to the household in the process."

I could see the care with which my stepfather had planned this, and how he would have smiled as he lowered the bucket, watching as it disappeared into the blackness with its precious cargo hooked over the side. He would have unwound the rope as slowly as he could, in order to make sure it did not swing against the side and dislodge the Broken Sword – for he would want me to believe it could be rescued – and be most noisy in the attempt.

"Then what is to do?" asked Sir John.

I thought through our possible options – each more fanciful than the last – and dismissed them all. For in truth, I knew there was but one way we could retrieve the Broken Sword, and I was being a fool to myself if I thought otherwise. It was full of danger and had no guarantee of success, but it was the only way.

"One of us must be tied by the feet to a separate rope," I said quietly, "and lowered head-first into the well, to find the sword and bring it up by hand."

"In Christ's name, no!" he exclaimed. "In the pitch dark and total silence? That is nigh impossible!"

"Can you think of a better way?" I asked.

There was another silence as he thought. Then he said, with a slight catch in his voice as if he was talking more to himself than to me, "I will do it. I will go down. It is my talisman – I must retrieve it."

How noble, that he would prefer to put himself in such danger than allow me to do so. Truly, his behaviour was that of a loving father. But however noble his intent, his proposal was not practical or sensible.

"No," I said softly. "I am half your weight and half your strength. One of us must hold the rope against the weight of the other going down. Which is best, the weaker person holds the heavier, or the stronger person holds the lighter?"

"Robert is light," he answered. "It could be him going down."

"Would you trust him?"

Once again there was a silence. I imagined the look of anguish on his face as he thought this through. "Very well," he said eventually. "You go down and I will hold you on the rope."

"It is agreed," I said. "There is rope in the old storeroom at the back of the house. Come."

I felt for his hand and led him cautiously along the passage and up the stairs. We came into the upper corridor and made our way quickly towards the far end. As we got closer to the dull light of the kitchen embers, I was able to see Sir John's face for the first time. His beard was untrimmed and his hair was unkempt, and even in the orange glow I could see how pale and grey he was. My anger at my stepfather and Sir Reginald burned as hot as the kitchen coals – this was an innocent man being badly used, just to gain advantage over me.

Well, they would not succeed.

They must not succeed.

I led Sir John out into the gardens. The moon had come out from behind clouds and was casting deep shadows around the grounds, making Marchington Manor look more menacing than ever. Truly I would only be content when we were away from its brooding bulk and free on the path towards Suffolk.

We used the blankets to make our way across the pebbled pathway like silent shadows, then ran quietly on the grass around the house till we came to where a storehouse was standing, old and unloved, behind some trees. I carefully pushed the door open wide and let the moonlight flood into the space. I smiled as I saw the rope curled up in a corner. It was where I had left it after making good my escape from the house one fine summer's day, but a few weeks ago.

Was it only a few weeks ago? It seemed like a lifetime.

I recalled it was the day that young Francis de Courtney and I had decided we would have the best of fun; we would disguise ourselves as peasants and dive for oysters in the Blackwater estuary. Unfortunately I had made the mistake of showing my rough smock and confiding my plan to the youngest of my three brothers, Henry. He, like a cloth-headed fool, had let it slip to Sir Andrew and I had been confined to my room with the door locked fast on me.

Henry had then come to my door to say how sorry he was, and when I had finished chiding him as roundly as any sister would, I told him he could make amends by fetching the rope from the old storehouse. This he did, passing the end of it under my door.

"How long will you be gone, Mary?" he asked from outside, once I had pulled the rope through.

"The full day," I answered.

"Will you be back for supper? Sir Andrew will expect you to attend," he paused, "in a gown."

"Most likely I will attend," I said. "Although I cannot promise to be so dressed."

There was a silence, so I thought he might have stepped softly away. Then he spoke again.

"Mary – Richard, Edward and me – we are most concerned for you."

"Indeed?" I asked, wondering where this was going.

"Aye. We were talking of this only today." He paused, and I could imagine him pulling at his ear, as he always did when thinking hard. "Edward says you should now step into line, and become a proper lady. He is starting to move in society, and he says he is embarrassed that people say his sister is wild and…" he paused again, "and uncontrolled."

"Uncontrolled? I would not be controlled by Sir Andrew."

"I know, and we have felt sorry for the way he treats you, but now, enough is enough." He paused again. "Mary, you really need to behave now. The three of us wish it, as your brothers."

"And yet you three continue to teach me to fight with a sword?"

"Yes, and we have taught you well. Too well, perhaps. And we agreed, that has got to stop. It is time for you end this pretence of being our brother, and become instead our loving sister, and marry Sir Reginald. It would be so much easier for us all."

"Easier for you three, you mean?" I muttered, tying the end of the rope to my bed post and opening the window. "But not for me." I took hold of the rope and stepped back onto the window ledge. "I will see you anon, Henry."

As I ran to join Francis down at Maldon's Hythe harbour, my feeling was of sadness rather than anger, that my brothers had now moved to the side of my stepfather. Where once I had three amiable playmates, who would support me when I needed, now I was but one against four; four men who expected me to be their perfect woman and wife to that monster.

But by the time I reached the harbour I was in a better mood, putting such dark thoughts aside for the day, ready to enjoy the adventure with Francis.

We met at the quay. "So, Mary," he said, greeting me with a mischievous smile, "what is your pleasure?"

"It is to have fun and to forget my family for a while," I answered.

"Mine too," he said, and we stood together a moment, taking in the sights, sounds and smells of the quay. There were many boats and ships lined up before us – some just arrived and unloading cargoes of spices and silks; some about to set off, with their sails raised and ready. We ran from one to the other, looking for a small fishing vessel, and eventually we came across just such a boat, with a weather-beaten old man and a young boy of around ten years sitting aboard.

"We would go to the oyster beds," I called to them.

"Aye, that is where we are bound," replied the old man. "Osea Island."

"Can we join you?" asked Francis. "We would dive for oysters."

The old man looked us up and down; seeing only a peasant boy and girl in rough clothing.

"Half your catch. That is the fare," he said.

"That is agreed," I answered, and we leapt aboard.

We had a fruitful day's diving, securing enough oysters to share half with the fisherman, whose name was Tom, and his grandson Septimus, and still have enough for our own pleasure.

We were a tired, but happy crew that docked again in Maldon that evening, and after a brief farewell to Francis, I made my way back to Marchington clutching a bag full of fresh oysters. Fortunately the rope was still where I had left it, and I was able to reach my room, hide the oysters and resume my normal clothes – or at least something more womanly – before my stepfather eventually came to release me.

I greeted him with an open and innocent smile, and although there was a brief frown on his face when he must have caught the slight salty smell of the oysters lingering in the air, he said nothing, but simply stood aside to let me out.

Yes – that was only a few weeks ago, but so much had changed. Poor Francis was dead, my brothers had made it clear they no longer supported me, and I was embarked on this madcap rescue – of a man I had known for but a few short days. All so I could leave Marchington Manor, my stepfather and Sir Reginald forever.

God willing.

I picked up the rope from the back of the storehouse and we made our way silently to the well. It stood in a small courtyard further round the house; a decrepit structure of worn brick topped by a shingle roof. The old capstan was slung below the roof, with a splintery wooden handle set into its side. The moonlight gave it a ghostly, malevolent air, like a foul spirit from the Underworld that was forced up though the ground to entrap us. I shivered, though the night was far from cold, and I forced myself not to think of the horror of descending down into the cold darkness.

Sir John stared at it, his mouth set in a grim line in the weak light of the moon. "Are you certain you will do this, Mary?" he asked. "Perchance the Broken Sword is hidden somewhere else, and your bravery will go unrewarded."

Nay," I answered. "See the rope – it is fully unwound, so the bucket must be as far down as it will go." I turned to him in the moonlight. "What other explanation for a disused well, than there is something down there?"

I walked to the edge of the well and peered over; my fear rising with bile in my throat. Fighting it down, I looked back at Sir John. "Come," I said in my most determined voice, "let us do this."

He passed the rope over the capstan, tied it securely to my legs, then tied the free end round his waist. I stood by the side of the well with my hands braced on the edge. He moved back to take up the slack, then I felt my legs being pulled out from under me. I supported myself by my arms as he pulled my legs higher and higher – then with a small cry I was fully suspended over the well, head down and with my hair hanging past my face.

I was now swinging freely over the terrible void. Behind me I could just make out the upside-down figure of Sir John holding the rope in front of his waist, braced against my weight.

With sickening terror I looked down into the well.

Truly it looked as black as Lucifer's heart.

I scarcely had time to ready myself before I felt myself lurch downwards and start to descend.

For all I was trying so hard to keep quiet, I heard myself let out another small cry as I dropped below the edge of the well.

Then the world turned completely black.

8

—————

CHAPTER EIGHT

If Hell is cold, black and stinking, and not red with fire and heat as they say, then the old well at the back of Marchington Manor was indeed the very essence of Hell itself.

My resolve to complete this task started to waver as soon as the weak moonlight of the night sky disappeared above my feet, and total darkness wrapped its cold hands about me. And with every jerking inch I descended, my doubts started to grow strong, like black ravens that feed on fear.

What if the sword was not even in the bucket? I had so easily assumed it would be, but maybe my stepfather had laid a more cunning plan. Maybe it was even now nestling beneath his pillow while he slept, his happy dream of his troublesome stepdaughter being removed forever on a poor fool's errand causing a smile to play across his sleeping face...

Or maybe it was indeed in the bucket, but how could I begin to believe I could find it and grasp it with the gentle touch needed to stop it dislodging from its perch and plunging to the bottom of the well – and to do this in the blackest of darkness while hanging by my feet…?

While these doubts grew, I continued to descend.

How deep was I now? Surely I must be near the bucket? I gave another little cry; perhaps I had already passed it! I had failed the errand and soon would plunge head-first into the putrid waters at the bottom of the well!

Blindly I put out my hand, hoping to find the well rope and reassure myself that I was not yet at the bucket.

But instead my hand touched cold, slimy brick. With a grunt of disgust, I contorted my body to turn it round, and quickly my hand found the taut central cable.

With a small feeling of relief, I continued downwards, with my hand running lightly along the rope.

After what seemed like many minutes – though in truth it must have been but a few short moments – my doubts started to return. Surely I could not need to go any further – how long was this wretched cord?

Perhaps there really was no bucket…

Instead I would continue down and down until the foul waters closed over my head. Then the last thing I would know as my hands touched a rock or stone or somesuch object weighting down the end of the well rope and my poor chest burst open – the last thing I would know before I drowned, was that my stepfather had won…

This vision seemed so real to me, I nearly choked on bile that once again flooded my mouth.

That was the moment when I was so close to abandoning the task.

I knew had only to make three short shakes on the rope with my feet – our pre-arranged signal – and Sir John would cease to walk slowly forward. Three more shakes and he would start to haul me back up again.

I would have to say I had found the bucket, and found it empty…

But God would see me lie. God would know. But at least I would be in the land of the living, not too early arrived in Heaven with Him. I would be back in the soft, beautiful moonlight and fresh air… By the Holy Cross, God would surely forgive me…

I could not imagine anything so welcome as emerging out of this well.

Except, perhaps, the look on Sir John's face as I held out the Broken Sword to him…

And perhaps also the look on my stepfather's face, if he found it gone…

So I did not send the signal. Instead I carried on down.

And further down.

Then God smiled on me for my honesty, for my hand touched a knot, then a metal handle.

Immediately I gave three shakes on the rope connecting me to Sir John, and my descent ceased.

Slowly, with care, I felt down the handle until I reached the side of the bucket. Then I started to feel round the side, which definitely sloped away at an angle.

That could only mean the sword was on the other side.

Still working with the smallest of movements, I ran my hand further round the rim of the bucket, until – oh Lord be praised! – my fingers touched something.

Holding my breath, I ran my fingers slowly along, feeling this object, touching it with the gentlest touch, praying it was indeed the Broken Sword.

My fingers traced around the edge of a guard, then up the jewelled handle…

It was indeed the sword!

And as I thought, it was perched precariously outside the bucket, with just the guard hooked over to hold it in place. I had been right about how my stepfather had planned this!

In my moment of triumph, I extended my fingers, meaning to grip the handle and secure it in my hand, but at that very moment, Sir John must have lost his footing, for suddenly I dropped again.

It was only a few inches – before Sir John no doubt secured himself – but it was enough to cause my hand to strike the Broken Sword.

With a dreadful grating sound that resonated on the rim of the bucket and echoed all around the well, the Broken Sword started to slide off.

With an anguished cry, I grabbed blindly at the space where I could hear it fall.

And caught it.

I had it only between my thumb and finger, with no real strength in the grip and already I could feel its weight start to pull itself from me.

I grasped the side of the bucket with my free hand and pulled the sword towards it, just as it slipped from my fingers and fell.

Into the bucket.

The clanging sound it made as it landed seemed loud

enough to wake the dead – but I could not worry about that when the sword saved!

I reached into the bucket and gripped it by the handle as tight as I could, then kicked three times again with my feet.

Holding the sword in the dark below me like a triumphant crusader, I felt myself being pulled up inch by painful inch by the worthy Sir John. I warrant he was now finding it much harder work to pull my weight up the well. Indeed, each time I looked up beyond my feet to the circle of moonlight that could just be seen against the blackness of the well, I swear it got no bigger.

But eventually I could see it had enlarged, and was now growing wider with every pull – until finally I could just make out the dry bricks at the top of the well in the soft light, and then – oh Heaven be praised! – I emerged from its confines into the welcome night.

Sir John was standing close, appearing to hang suspended by his feet from the upside-down ground, the rope around his back. As I emerged, he reached to pull me to the edge of the well. With a soft, but triumphant cry I announced, "I have it!" and I held out the Broken Sword.

I think he would have forgot himself and let me go in his eagerness to grasp the object from me – and indeed I did drop a few inches with an alarmed squeak before he quickly secured the rope in his free hand, but thank God I did not go plummeting back down that dreadful black hole once again. Instead he took the sword and dropped it on the ground, pulled me across the lip of the well, then let the rope play out so I could land, gasping like a fisherman's catch, on the dark earth by the well.

He untied my legs and I struggled dizzily to my feet, clutching at the side of the well for support.

"Bravo, Mistress Mary!" he whispered, the smile on his face as broad as I could have hoped. "You have done fine work down that hellish hole."

"And you," I answered. "You pulled well."

"But I could not have done…" he began, but I waved my hand for silence.

"Fie!" I admonished. "There will be time enough for congratulations when we three are away from this cursed manor. We must find Wee… Robert… and get to the horses!"

"Aye," he agreed, and began curling up the rope. "I shall throw this down the well."

"Perhaps!" I answered. "Or perhaps leave it by the well so Sir Andrew and Sir Reginald will see it. Then they will know what we have done. They will realise that we have won – that when they pull that bucket up, the Broken Sword will be gone."

He smiled slowly in the moonlight. "Aye, that is a better course of action. Then that is what we will do." He hung the coiled rope over the handle and stood back to admire how clearly it would be seen. "Now come," he said. "Where do we find my son?"

9

CHAPTER NINE

I must confess, my heart was in my mouth as we crept silently back across the gravel path on the blankets. Would Weed have been able to maintain his deception as this counterfeit soldier called Rob Godfrey long enough to complete his part of the plan? As a young man with smooth skin and sandy hair, his deception was easy enough in the dark, but would the tallow candlelight in old Tom's watchman's hut make his crudely blackened face and chalk-grey hair painfully obvious? I prayed that Tom had but one candle lit, and that there were sufficient shadows for Weed to keep from being seen too clearly.

The hut was no more than a rough wooden structure with a thatched roof leaning up against the wall to one of the gardens. As we came up to it, I indicated to Sir John to stay back so I could approach alone.

Cautiously I approached from the side, then dropped into

a crouch and peered slowly round the base of the rough wooden door.

The hut was pitch black; no light emanating from it at all. I stared for a couple of minutes into the inky darkness, until my eyes became accustomed, and I made out a figure slumped over the table.

I held my breath, then started to creep slowly inside. I was nearly at the table, when a sudden sound made me jump.

It was the sound of a man's snore.

I crept closer, until I could make out the figure of old Tom collapsed onto his arms; a pewter cup knocked over beside him with a small spill of liquid coming from it. I dipped my finger in the liquid and sniffed; it was definitely rum.

So Weed had succeeded in getting Tom drunk. This was excellent work, as it meant that Tom would hardly admit to his dereliction of duty, if he even remembered it at all, and my rescue of Sir John and the Broken Sword would remain unknown until my stepfather either happened on the rope by the well, found Sir John gone, or questioned why the dogs were locked up – which would be enough time for us to be many miles from Marchington Manor.

But what of Weed?

Our plan had been simple. Once he had assured himself Tom was no longer able to raise the alarm, he was to take the keys from the old man and make his way back to the gate. I smiled to myself. So it had all gone to plan; his absence must have meant that he had succeeded! We were as good as away from this cursed house!

Then I heard a different snore.

It was the sound of a thinner, younger man, and it came from the shadows deep in the corner of the hut. As I peered into the dark recess, the moon came out briefly from behind a cloud, revealing Weed slumped against the wall; an empty cup resting against his limp hand.

With a muttered curse I slipped out from the hut, to find Sir John standing anxiously just outside.

"What of my son? he whispered.

"The fool has got himself drunk," I answered, "and is still here, sleeping like a babe."

"Devil take him," he muttered. Then he looked hard at me. "What is to be done?"

"We cannot leave him," I said. "So we will have to either wake him or carry him away."

We entered the hut, and I crouched low beside the sleeping Weed. Gently I slapped his face. "Wake up, fool," I growled, but he remained unconscious. I slapped a little harder, with the same result.

"We must carry him out," Sir John muttered. I nodded, then pulled Weed round until I could get my hands under his arms. His father grabbed his legs, and together we lifted him up.

"Wait!" I hissed. "We must do as he should have done, and take the key to the gate."

We dropped Weed back to the floor, where he lay without further movement.

I turned to old Tom. Although he was fallen across the table, I hoped the keys would be at his belt, where I might reach them with some ease. I waited till the moon came once again, casting its eerie light across the inside of the hut and either lighting up parts in silvery blue or throwing them in the deepest black shadow. I peered at Tom's belt, but saw no keys, so I crept around the back of his bench to his other side. Here everything was in shadow, so I put out my hand and touched as lightly as I could to where I thought was his leg. I found nothing that had the feel of a key, just rough woollen breeches, so I moved my hand ever upwards... until the welcome feel of cold metal met my fingers.

Holding my breath, I grasped the keys and lifted them up, hoping he had them on a simple hook. But as I lifted, Tom must have felt the movement in his sleep, and, with a grunt, he moved his position.

Gradually I released my breath. With the greatest good fortune, this movement had actually released the keys! Triumphantly I crawled back to the other side, hooking the keys over my own belt as I went.

"I have them!" I hissed. Once again we lifted the sleeping Weed and started to carry him out.

Tom's table was all that lay between us and the door – to get out, we must carry Weed most carefully, so as not to knock into it and wake the old man. Sir John soon cleared it with Weed's feet, so that all I must do was get his upper body and head past. Gripping him as tight as I could, I shuffled along, praying Weed would not move.

Unfortunately, God chose to ignore my prayer.

As we passed the table, he gave a loud groan, and suddenly his arm flew out beside him, causing his hand to crash down onto the table with the sound of a canon firing.

Immediately Tom shook his head and sat up. There was a moment when he stared at me in the moonlight with a look that plainly said he was not understanding what he was seeing, then it was as if a candle was lit up behind his eyes as he recognised me.

He gave a great bellow of rage.

"Mistress Fox!" he yelled. "By Heaven, 'tis Mistress Fox!" He reached across the table and suddenly there was a hand bell clutched in his fist, and loud peals broke out across the still night as he shook it mightily.

Now there was no need for silence, so I shouted to Sir John, "Haste, haste!" and together we carried Weed out of the hut and set off as fast as we could towards the gate.

Behind me, I could hear the crash of a bench falling as Tom must have staggered to his feet, then a further crash and a yell as he must have lost his balance and fallen over – no doubt with the sudden dizziness from the rum he had drunk.

By then we were covering the ground as fast as we could, despite carrying the still-sleeping Weed between us.

Again I heard the pealing of the bell, sounding loud enough to wake every person in Essex, accompanied by loud shouts from Tom.

"Mistress Fox! Mistress Fox is here!"

But it was not the worthy county folk that he woke, it was my stepfather.

As we came closer to the gate, I heard his familiar bellow, sounding for all the world like a bull sighting a prize heifer, and in terror I glanced round, to see him come out of the house and run down the steps, carrying a lantern.

As I did so, Weed awoke, and in his confused state, he tried to wriggle from my arms. I attempted to hang onto him, but he twisted too far, and I was forced to let go. With a loud crack, his head hit the ground. I yelped, "Robert! No!" and Sir John shouted, "Pick him up, quick!" I did so, seeing that Weed was once again unconscious, just as my stepfather started to run towards us. Strangely, he was fully dressed. Even as I ran I was thinking that he must have slept in his clothes, ready for just this eventuality.

I turned back and shouted again to Sir John, "Haste! We must make the gates!" But Weed was dead weight in our arms, and Sir John was running backwards carrying Weed's feet, so we could make but a quarter of the pace my stepfather was making.

I could feel the ground shake with the pounding of his feet as he chased after us, and even though I could now see the gates clearly before me in the moonlight, it seemed only the slimmest chance that we could reach them before we were caught.

The thought of being dragged back into that cursed house, thrown into my room behind the locked door, then being forced to wed that vile Sir Reginald, made me feel as if I would be physically sick.

I had to try everything I could to stop that happening.

"Run!" I screamed to Sir John. He could see my stepfather advancing behind me, and this terrifying vision gave him the sudden turn of extra speed we needed, so that we made it to the gates while Sir Andrew was still some twenty yards behind.

Dropping Weed down with, I must admit, small care again for his head, I grabbed the keys from my belt and selected the one that looked most likely to fit the lock. With another prayer I thrust it into the lock and turned.

Once again, it seemed God was not on my side, as the key would not turn.

I glanced back. My stepfather was no more than ten yards away, bellowing once again like a bull – only this time it was the triumphant sound of a bull about to grab its victim.

With a scream of rage, I tried the next key, and this time God took my part. The key turned and I pushed the gate open. Then I grabbed Weed and together Sir John and I dragged him through the gate.

Again I dropped him, then turned and slammed the gate shut, just as my stepfather reached it. Before he could turn the latch, I slipped the key back in and locked it fast.

There was a moment as Sir Andrew stared deep into my eyes through the iron bars, and I swear he snarled like a dog.

"You will not get away with this, Mary," he growled, gripping the bars with white hands as I moved back, away from his reach. "You will not defy me in such an unnatural way."

I said nothing.

"I will find you, and do you know what I will do?"

Again I did not answer.

"Either I will drag you back to Marchington Manor bound in ropes to be married as a dutiful daughter, or..." he paused, his eyes burning into mine, "or I will punish you for your disobedience and your dishonour to my name." He leaned forward, until his face was framed between the bars. "Oh yes, if you defy me in this, I will punish you, Mary Fox, you wilful woman." He smiled, a slow, evil smile, but it was clear he was not joking. "Do you know what I will do?"

I held his gaze without making any reaction, as I could not trust myself not to scream at him like a demented banshee.

"I will kill you."

I felt sure I would soon be sick, but managed to maintain my stare. Taking a steadying breath, I answered as levelly as I could, "Then I had better make sure you do not catch me, father dear."

We continued to stare at each other for a moment more, almost like some childish game, then he deliberately spat on the ground, turned and stalked away from the gate, over to where I now saw Sir Reginald was standing, also fully clothed, holding another lantern.

We picked up the still unconscious Weed, threw him across the back of his horse, then mounted ourselves.

"Your tales of your stepfather did not do justice to his evil," observed Sir John as we rode away from that cursed place.

I still felt too sick to find words, and he accepted my silence as response enough.

Beside me, Weed lay prostrate across his horse's back, bouncing like a bag of wheat as we galloped through the forest. Was he now just asleep from the amount of rum he had drunk, or was he still unconscious from the many times I had dropped him heavily on his thick head?

Either way, by the time we arrived at the yard of the Blue Boar in Maldon, he was thankfully awake, groaning and eying me with some disfavour.

I slipped off Hestia and crouched by his head. "By all that is holy," I said, finding my voice now we were well away from Marchington Manor and murderous stepfathers, "what were you doing, drinking rum to the point of oblivion?"

He regarded me a moment with a bloodshot eye, then

muttered, "The man challenged me to keep with him, drink for drink. What could I do?"

"Pretend!" I yelled. "You could have pretended! You did not need to drain every draft!"

"Yes, well, you were not there."

"No," I answered, standing. "I was otherwise engaged, retrieving your precious Broken Sword." I walked over to where his father was unsaddling his horse. "Your son lives," I muttered. Behind me I heard a yelp and a thumping noise, and turned to see that Weed had slithered off his horse's back and was now lying unconscious again on the cobbles alongside its hooves. "And has now dismounted."

Sir John grunted his acknowledgement and went over to tend to his son, while I unsaddled my own mount and led her to a stable.

10

CHAPTER TEN

"We must not delay our departure for Nacton another moment," I observed, as Sir John and I sat by the roaring fire in the parlour of the Blue Boar inn a short while later, seeking to warm ourselves after our flight from Marchington Manor. Weed was curled up on the floor at our feet where we had dropped him, still in the same unconscious state. "My stepfather is unlikely to return to his bed for the night," I added, "but will no doubt even now be gathering his men and preparing to track us across Essex." My body gave a chill shiver despite the warmth of the fire, as once again I saw his evil face through the bars, and heard him snarl, "Oh yes, if you defy me in this, I will punish you, Mary Fox, my wilful girl… I will kill you."

This was no idle threat. My fate if brought back to Marchington, no doubt pulled behind a horse like Sir John, would be either marriage or death. So I had no option but to press on to Nacton and protection under Sir John's roof as quickly as possible, rather than face that awful situation.

I looked down at the curled-up body beside me.

"We must find a way to wake Robert and make him fit to ride out, and most presently," I observed, and Sir John nodded.

"Aye, 'tis most pressing that we leave this place, but…" he stole a glance down at his son, with a look on his face that seemed to combine both pity and disappointment, "…he is unused to such strong drink. I would not expect him to be fit to ride for many an hour yet."

"We must keep moving," I snapped. I realised I had been very sharp, so I added quickly, "if we are to get the Broken Sword back to your family." I looked down at Weed again.

"Aye," Sir John said, as he gazed deeply into the fire, his eyes reflecting the bright orange dance of the flames. "Although I hope that by simply having the totem in my possession, the curse might be reduced by even a small measure." He turned to me with a steady, resolute look. "But you are right as always, Mary Fox, and we must wake him one way or another and move on."

I nodded in relieved agreement; he did not seem to have taken offence. I told myself I must keep an even temperament; it was as much in Sir John's interest to make our escape, as it was in mine. Which would best happen if only we could wake Weed up.

I eyed the large pitcher of thin ale on the table, and considered to myself what would be the effect of emptying it over him. I turned back to Sir John, and he smiled; clearly understanding exactly what I intended.

"I concur, my dear Mary, we should answer drink with more drink, but poured onto his thick head, rather than into it."

I nodded, as suddenly he frowned. "But then what?" he asked. "How do we then keep a step ahead of our pursuers all the way to Nacton?"

I took a slow breath. "I have given that much thought, believe me." Indeed, this vexing question had been foremost in my mind ever since we had ridden from the gates of Marchington. I had considered it from every angle, and could see only one way we could achieve our goal. But first I had a question. "Nacton is by the sea, is it not?"

He nodded. "It is by the River Orwell, not more than a few leagues from the open sea at Harwich."

"Then perhaps we can find a boat out of Maldon and make our way by water?" I said. "There are boats out of the harbour at all times, and I have no doubt some will leave at first light." This I knew from my adventure with poor Francis only a few weeks ago, although a voyage up the coast to Nacton would be quite a different journey to one diving for oysters off Osea Island. We would need a bigger boat, for one thing.

"But first we must get to the harbour unseen, then find a captain willing to take us," he said, voicing the very concern that had been troubling me also. "There is much we are leaving to fate." He paused a moment, then added, "The sooner we set off, the more time we have to find such a captain."

As one, we both turned to look at the sleeping man at our feet. "I suppose we had better try and wake him up now," he said slowly, and again he looked at the pitcher of ale.

It had been left for us by the innkeeper. This good fellow

had remained mercifully silent when I had wakened him from his slumbers earlier and staggered in, accompanied by a strange older man and a comatose Weed. He had merely grunted acknowledgement that we had returned, accepted back his blankets, while ignoring Weed's chalk-streaked hair and dirt-covered face. He had then fetched some cups and the pitcher and padded back to his chamber.

I stood and picked it up, then slowly poured some ale onto Weed's head.

Nothing happened, except that the brown liquid washed some dirt off his face and into his ear. With an anxious glance at his father, I poured a bit more. Now the stream tracked the dirt down his cheek and into the side of his mouth, but still there was no response.

"Here, let me," said Sir John, taking the pitcher. He poured it harder, so the liquid landed on the side of his son's head with some force. Soon it was empty, and I held my breath as I sought signs of life.

After what seemed like an age, Weed gave a small cough, then was silent. We watched for further movement, exchanging frequent nervous glances, and were eventually rewarded with another cough.

"Robert?" I said. "Do you hear me?"

Weed groaned; a low, short sound like a young ox in some pain.

"Come, Robert, wake up now," Sir John commanded.

Weed groaned again, and his eyelids fluttered. Then they opened like two rusty trapdoors to reveal pinprick red eyes, which stared balefully at us both.

"Leave me alone," he muttered.

Sir John crouched down beside him. "Come son, you must awake," he said, in a tone which was kinder than I felt the situation warranted. "We must be away from this place and quickly."

Weed continued to stare at his father through slit eyes. Sir John tried again. "Come, son. We have little time to lose. There are men coming even now who mean us great harm."

Weed turned his head and regarded me, then looked back at his father.

"So she succeeded then?" he whispered. "She got you away from that place?"

Sir John smiled. "Aye, she did that. And with much thanks to you for distracting the guard."

"And they come in vengeance, even now?"

"They do."

Weed gave another low groan. "My head hurts."

"There will be time enough to recover, once we are away from here."

Then Weed did something which I had not expected. With great effort he struggled to his feet, putting one hand to the table as if to stop himself falling back to the floor. He gave me a weak smile. "We did well, Mary Fox, did we not?" He coughed, then put his other hand to his head with a brief grimace. "We fooled old Tom, so he thought I was a comrade." He paused. "I did not have to say anything; I just had to nod as he talked. And I had to drink, too; he was most insistent." His lower lip trembled slightly. "I am so sorry, Mary, I really am. I did mean not to drink as I am barely used to strong liquor, but he opened another bottle and filled my cup each time... and he watched me drink most carefully."

He looked such a piteous figure, with streaks of ale running through the dirt on his face and the chalk lines in his hair, that he reminded me of a sad old badger. Indeed, he looked so pitiful that I could no longer find it in my heart to be cross with him.

"'Tis no matter," I said, with a small smile. "The main thing is that we are all together, with a chance to get the Broken Sword back to your mother and sister."

"Then let us go now," he said, stepping away from the table. This seemed too sudden a movement, as he staggered and put his hand quickly back to steady himself. Sir John moved forward. "Come, Robert," he said, placing his arm round the boy's waist, "I will hold you."

Together we made our way out of the parlour and into the cool night air.

11

CHAPTER ELEVEN

The dawn sky was glowing a rosy pink behind the masts and sails of the boats moored in Maldon's Hythe Quay, as we walked down from the town.

There had been little to do to make good our departure from the Blue Boar, other than to settle our account with the landlord, who we had once again roused from his slumbers, to thank him for his help, and to say goodbye to my horse, Hestia. I had spent a last few precious minutes in her company, stroking her neck and feeding her some oats as she stood in the stables, her dark eye glinting in the moonlight as if she knew that we were about to part.

"I will seek you out, old girl," I said. "I must go now by sea and I cannot take you with me, but one day I will find you again, and we shall be together once more."

She gave a little whinny.

Again I stroked her neck. "I shall miss you," I said. "We

have had some adventures together, have we not?" She shook her head up and down, as if agreeing with me.

"I have asked the landlord to find you a good home; someone who will love and care for you as much as I have."

She whinnied again. "Such a person will be there for you, my love," I said, "And I will one day find you again and get you back." She fixed her eye on me and snorted gently. "That is a promise." I stroked her soft velvet muzzle for a moment, then stood back. "Goodbye, Hestia," I said, and slipped out of the stable.

And now we were down at Maldon's Hythe Quay, looking to get on our way.

Despite the early hour, the quay was a mass of activity; men moving on and off boats carrying all manner of bags, barrels, sails and spars; small boys scurrying about barefoot; taverns and inns with light spilling from the doors and windows; women inside kissing goodbye to their menfolk; shouts of captains calling to their crews, and a few larger vessels already moving slowly away from the quayside with their sails flapping and cracking as they started to fill with wind.

I turned to Sir John. "We should aim for medium-sized boats," I said.

He nodded. "Large enough to be going up the coast, but not so large as to be crossing open water to the low countries."

We made our way down to the dock, with Weed staggering along behind us, groaning and clutching at his head. I looked along the line of boats with their bows hard up against the dockside. Each was secured by a stout rope to a black chain as thick as my waist, running the length of the dock. The larger ones had a long wooden bowsprit pushing out beyond the bow, soaring overhead like the branch of a majestic tree. I walked on past these, as they would be the ones crossing the open waters. Soon we came to medium-sized vessels, their sails flapping idly. Men were walking up and down gangplanks with barrels on their backs or carrying bulging canvas bags, no doubt full of cargo, or provisions for the voyage.

I spied a couple of likely-looking vessels. Each was around forty feet in length, with two masts, a small bow-castle like a fenced-off platform, and a larger raised section at the stern that I took to hold the captain's quarters and other cabins. The one on the left had the figure of a painted mermaid gracing its bow, while the one on the right had a long-beaked bird with its open wings wrapped around the sides of the hull. I grasped Sir John's sleeve and pointed, and again he nodded.

"You must ask for passage," I said. "I doubt they would listen to a woman such as I."

"Indeed," he answered, "many sailors consider a woman on board their boat is a bringer of bad fortune." He stopped and looked carefully at me. "You are still dressed in the jerkin and breeches of a peasant boy, as you were last night."

"I have not had the chance to change," I observed. "Nor would I wish to, for as I have said, I do not feel comfortable in the clothes that society says I should wear – it is one of the many failings that pains my stepfather so."

He looked at my hair, which was unconstrained by any hood and flowed freely over my shoulders. "Then for the purposes of this voyage, you are a boy – and like to remain so," he said, "and your loose hair adds truth to this deception."

Weed muttered, "It is not natural."

His father turned on him. "Nay," he snapped, "it is not natural. But it may well help us get the Broken Sword back to your mother and sister, so it is well that it is so."

As Weed fell back into a pained silence, I glanced quickly at him. The Weed of the previous night who had begged my forgiveness now seemed to have gone, to be replaced once more by the truculent young man. I decided to see if this would be short-lived, or if I would need to re-build our relationship once more.

Sir John motioned us to stay back, then he approached the first vessel, making his way along the wooden jetty that ran out from the dockside like a deep valley between the sides of the two ships. We saw him call up to a man on the deck, but could not see the man or hear the words. Sir John must have had a negative answer, as he then turned and called up to another man on the second ship. A head appeared over the side and they conversed a while, then Sir John walked back to us.

"The captain on the second ship says he will take us as far as Harwich," he announced. "He says his ship, which is called the *Curliewe*, leaves in no more than an hour, and asks us to board a few minutes beforehand, once he has finished loading his cargo of wool for Norwich." He smiled. "I told him we were a father, son and serving lad." He looked hard at me, his smile gone as suddenly as it came. "That is you, sweet Mary, so you had best not be issuing your orders, or even talking too much, lest they see you as the forceful girl you are, and not as a humble lad."

There was a snort from Weed at this. "'Tis much to hope for," he muttered.

Sir John either did not hear this, or chose to ignore it. "Once we are in Harwich, the captain says we will easily find a second boat to take us up the River Orwell to Nacton. He says the journey to Harwich will take around ten hours, as the wind is from the south west and the tide will be on the wane when we depart."

"And he will not let us embark now?" I asked. "We would keep out of sight as much as we can, and the ship is the ideal place."

"Nay," he answered, "he says that loading the cargo is the most important thing, and he worries we would be in the way."

This was blow to my plans, for every moment we were on the dockside we could be seen by my stepfather or Sir Reginald. "And he would not be moved on this?"

"Nay. I did not want to press the point, for fear of seeming desperate."

I could see that this was sensible; if the captain thought we were on the run for our lives, he might consider us too much of a risk and refuse to give us passage. "Then we must find a place to keep our heads down for an hour," I said, and Sir John nodded.

I looked around, trying to identify any figure who looked like the stick-like shape of Sir Reginald, or men whose business on the quay was to seek fugitives rather than heed the call of the sea, but amongst the crowds of men every one seemed to be hurrying to and fro as I imagined a genuine sailor would; slinging canvas bags over their shoulder or hefting barrels of drink.

"Come," I said, "let us find a quiet corner in that tavern and keep our heads low."

As we made our way over to the tavern, I fell in step beside Weed. It was clear that this bitterness between us would never be resolved unless one of us made the first move, and that it would have to be me that did so.

"How is your head?" I asked.

He walked on in silence, the head in question remaining bowed.

I tried again. "Are you feeling better?"

"'Tis no concern of yours," he muttered

"But it is my concern," I answered. "My concern is for your welfare."

"Like as not."

"Oh come, now," I said, putting some lightness into my voice, "I am doing all I can to help you restore your family's health and fortune by the return of the Broken Sword. If that is not concern for your welfare, then I do not know what is."

Fortunately, this last comment seemed to reach him. "I grant you are helping us," he began, then he paused a moment, as if seeking the right words. "But we help you also." He looked up with eyes that were still bloodshot. "We are helping you escape your stepfather and his plans for your marriage."

"Yes," I agreed, "and you must know how grateful I am."

"Hmm."

"And here we are now," I continued, "soon to begin our

voyage to return the Broken Sword to your home. And," I added, "I look to you for your help and support in this."

"I would have thought you would be chiding me at every turn," he said. "For being a coward and a drunken sot."

"And where would that get us?" I asked. "We have to work together, not apart, if we are to succeed in our mission."

His eyebrows shot up. "The great Mary Fox would forgive my failings?"

I smiled at him, to show his irony had bounced off me, like a sword off heavy armour. "Of course," I said, "we all have failings."

"And you delight in pointing out mine."

I considered this a moment. "You played your part of the old soldier well," I suggested.

At this he stopped and lifted his head, staring at me. "Yet because I was drunk the alarm was sounded and you were nearly caught."

"Aye," I answered, "but we got away, nonetheless. That is the most important part."

Weed started walking on again, to catch up Sir John as he entered the tavern. "Then let us work together, Mary Fox," he said over his shoulder, "if you will trust I will do my best to help."

"I will," I said, feeling as if a weight had lifted from my shoulders as we entered the tavern. "I will indeed."

The tavern was full of men, shouting across each other, roaring with laughter, clapping each other on the backs, drinking copious quantities of ale and eating hams and pies off wooden trenchers. We kept our heads low, as we made our way over to an empty table in the corner and took our seats with our backs as much as possible to the door. A serving girl came to our table and asked what we wanted. Sir John ordered some pie and ale, and asked for three further pies for our voyage. I observed the girl as she walked across the room, then disappeared through a door at the back. I caught a brief glimpse of the kitchens beyond, with an open doorway to the outside. I noted this carefully – it could be our escape route if needed.

The girl emerged some time later with the pies to eat now and the others wrapped in cloth packets, together with three tankards of ale.

As we ate I kept turning and watching the door with quick glances, in case Sir Reginald and his men were to come in, or Sir Andrew. It was one such time that I saw the door open and four men come in. Unlike the sailors filling the tavern, they each had a metal breastplate over mail shirts and were wearing kettle helmets. Just as I was studying these men and trying to decide if they were a threat, the door opened once again, and my blood ran cold as I stared at the thin and loathsome features of Sir Reginald de Courtney.

Quickly I turned back in case he should see my face. Sir John saw my reaction and hissed, "What ails Mary? Art white as a bedsheet."

"It is de Courtney," I hissed back. "We must be away as quiet as we can!"

Without a moment's hesitation Sir John grabbed the food packets and we all stood.

"This way!" I said pointing at the door at the back, and

together we started pushing through the throng towards it. Just as we got there, I heard a bellow from across the room, "Hie! Hie! There they are! Quick!"

Abandoning all hope of concealment, we ran for the door. I reached it first and burst through, into the small kitchens. I checked a moment, causing Sir John and Weed to cascade into my back, as I looked for the outside door, which was now closed. "There!" I pointed, then gathered myself and made for it in the greatest haste. The servants moved aside as we ran; no doubt they were used to fleeing sailors using their kitchens as a passage, and one even opened the door for us as we approached. We flew through it like birds on the wing and tumbled into a passageway outside the back of the tavern. I quickly pulled the door shut, but the latch was on the inside, so there was no way I could secure it against the might of Sir Reginald and his men.

"Come!" I yelled to Sir John and Weed, and started to run towards the end of the passageway, just as I heard the door open behind us and triumphant shouts of "Hie! Hie! Do not let them escape!"

We emerged into the bright morning sunshine close by the quayside. I stole a brief look at the lines of boats to our left and right, and marked the *Curliewe* by the carved bird on its bow. It was no more than a hundred paces away to our right; but we had Sir Reginald and his men close on our heels.

I caught sight of a stack of barrels standing on the quayside. A sudden idea formed, and I quickly changed direction, heading for these instead of the *Curliewe*. By good fortune both Sir John and Weed saw my change of direction and followed. We reached the stack of barrels and all leapt behind them. I gave a quick glance at Sir John and could see that he immediately understood my idea; then glanced over at Weed, and he too had grasped the essence of my plan.

All five men were close; in the briefest moment they would be upon us. With no time to spare, we pushed the top barrel off the pile so that it rolled forward, directly into the path of the oncoming men. It struck the legs of the first man, so he tumbled forward like a felled log. The two behind him then tripped over his prostrate body and crashed to the ground; the weight of their heavy breastplates pulling them down and stopping them from quickly getting back up.

The fourth man leapt across the bodies. He was followed by Sir Reginald, a look of evil triumph on his twisted face. At this I saw Weed beside me pick up a further barrel with both hands and lift it high.

"Enough of this," he growled as the man appeared round the side of our cover, then he gave a loud shout and brought the barrel crashing down on the fellow's head. Even though he wore a kettle helmet, the weight of the barrel was too much; his helmet was pushed hard onto his face and he went down like a sack of flour.

Sir John picked up a further barrel and held it aloft, ready for Sir Reginald. At this the older man checked a moment. No doubt he could see that to get any closer might expose him to the same fate as Weed's victim, and without a helmet to protect him, it would clearly be a much worse outcome.

This gave me time to draw my sword.

"Be gone, Sir Reginald," I yelled, putting as much menace into my voice as I could. "And take your men with you."

He stared at me with such loathing in his eyes that I could scarce countenance how he could ever possibly want to take me in marriage. Then he smiled, a cold, empty smile. "I shall not forget this, Mary Fox," he said. "When I have you in my power as my wife, I shall not forget that you have drawn your sword on me. I shall make you recall this moment every time I bend you to my will. I will never let it pass."

"What you forget is that we are not yet wed, Sir Reginald," I pointed out, "nor do I intend we should ever be."

"What you must remember, Mistress Mary Fox," he snapped back, "is that you are a mere girl, subject to your father's will. That is the law of the land, and you would do well to mark it, for I will have the weight of the law behind me when I take you into my house as my wife, as your father has determined."

I pushed the sword forward until the tip touched his doublet, just left of his breastbone. I saw him flinch slightly, for all that his eyes never left mine.

"I would sooner be arraigned and hung for your murder," I whispered, "than spend a single moment as your wife." I pushed a little more and he gave ground. "As I said just now, be gone and take your men with you."

There were a few moments when he stared at me across my blade, then his eyes narrowed, as he must have made his mind up to concede.

"I shall be gone for now, Mary Fox," he said, "but the next time we meet I will be ready, and you will not have a chance of escape." He backed away a few paces. "Mark that, girl," he snapped, "mark it well."

I said nothing, but kept my blade pointing forward.

"Come," he ordered his men, then turned and started to walk away. One by one they clambered to their feet and followed. This even included the one hit by Weed, who used both hands to push the helmet up to reveal a bloodied nose, then weaved unsteadily back after his master and companions and followed them into the tavern.

There was a moment's silence, then I sheathed my sword and turned to Weed. "By God, Master Robert, that was a magnificent blow! I am impressed!"

His father nodded as he put his barrel down. "Well done, son, that was excellently done."

I saw that Weed had started to breathe in short, sharp breaths, as if he had just run a hundred paces. "I… did… I… hit… him… did… I… not?" He tried to smile. "I… actually… did…"

"Yes," I said, putting my hand on his arm, "you did, and it was just what was needed."

His breathing slowed a little, as his other hand came to rest on top of mine.

"We must get to the *Curliewe* now," I said, gently pulling my hand out from under his. "It is close to the hour and she will sail soon."

12

CHAPTER TWELVE

The *Curliewe* was not a large ship; indeed she was no more than twenty short paces from bow to stern, but to me she was more magnificent than the Mary Rose herself, as she bore us majestically out of the mouth of the River Blackwater and into the open seas beyond.

I leant against the ship's rail, watching the sparkling waves cascade off the bow below me, feeling the boat start to rise and fall with the growing wind and the swell of the open water, and for the first time since I had decided to run away from Marchington Manor, I started to feel free.

But why should I be feeling so?

I looked across at the Essex coast, as if seeking inspiration from the muddy grey shoreline. I shook my head. In truth, a woman of my years from a fine family should be dreaming of one thing and one thing only; her every waking hour should be absorbed with thoughts of making a good marriage, ideally with a handsome, well-connected young man. She should be constructing in her mind a man that she would gladly spend the rest of her life with; imagining how he would value her as a loving and adoring wife, as keeper of his home and mother of his children.

And in truth, such thoughts did sometimes cross my mind; only to be replaced with ones of dark anger against my stepfather for making any such dream become a nightmare. Sir Andrew was clearly the devil incarnate, that he would treat the only daughter of his beloved wife so cruelly.

The unbroken line of the coast stretched across my view, with no hill, tree or dwelling to break up its monotony; indeed, it was so uninteresting that it brought to mind the man my stepfather so desired me to marry. How could he think to use me as a pawn in his game of ambition, ready to sacrifice my happiness by offering me to the dried-up old stick that was Sir Reginald?

But then, no!

No, no and thrice, no! I must not wallow in such self- pity!

The *Curliewe* was carrying me ever further from Sir Reginald, from my murderous stepfather and from of the bounds of servitude placed about me in Marchington Manor. I must look now to a life of happiness; a life without elderly men who would use me cruelly as their wife.

I glanced back along the boat, to where Weed and Sir John were standing, also by the rail.

Weed was a curiosity, that was for sure. He had shown nothing but cowardice until the night before, when he had taken on the part of an old soldier and carried it through, almost to a successful conclusion. Then today, with a head still full of drink, he had lifted a barrel and brought it down on a man with enough force to render him almost senseless. What had caused such a change of spirit?

Almost as if he knew I was observing him, Weed looked over at me, and gave a small smile. No doubt he was acknowledging that together we had nearly achieved our aim; we were close to restoring the Broken Sword to its rightful place, and with it, the health and prosperity of his family.

Was that the first time I had seen Weed smile? I smiled back, then had a surprising thought. Maybe Weed was not so weed-like after all?

I chewed on my lip as I stared at him. Was I starting to see him in a new light? Was the man who had hidden when his father was in danger, and who had allowed himself to be led all the while by a woman such as I, now starting to show a little spirit?

I studied his face as he narrowed his eyes and lifted his chin to the wind. I had once thought it rather a feeble face, but now I looked again, I could see there was perhaps a little more nobility in his brow than I had seen before. And maybe a slightly more pleasing shape to his mouth.

Maybe I should stop thinking of him as Weed, and bestow on him his proper name of Robert? Yes, that would be the right thing to do. By continuing to call him Weed, I was not allowing him to be anything else. So, from now on, he would be Robert. I nodded to myself, satisfied with this decision.

Then I looked across at Sir John, and I was shocked. He was looking pale, almost green with sickness. Even as I watched, he leaned over the rail and vomited twice.

Immediately I ran down to their deck, holding on tight to the rope that was fixed beside the steps as the *Curliewe* lurched and rolled ever more heavily in the freshening wind.

"What ails you, Sir John?" I asked.

He stood up and looked over his shoulder, his hands still gripping the rail with white knuckles.

"He is not used to the movement of the boat," said Weed… Robert.

The wind whipped around us as Sir John stood back from the rail. He wiped some flecks of vomit from his beard with his sleeve.

"The sea is too rough for me, dear Mary," he shouted against the increasing wind. "It so ails me that I must find my bunk and lie down, and try to sleep."

With that, he lurched unsteadily to the stern of the boat, and staggered through the door to the cabins.

I turned to Robert. "How do you fare?" I asked, now having to raise my voice to be heard.

"My head is clear of the drink," he answered, "if that is what you mean."

"In truth it was not," I shouted, with a smile. "I was concerned that you were not also feeling sick from the rock and roll of the boat."

"Nay, Mary," he called back, "my father has been holed up in a prison dungeon until yesterday – I think his body is not able to cope with all this movement."

"True," I shouted. "But it is becoming impossible to hear each other out here – let us seek shelter."

He nodded, and we made our way to the door down to

the cabins and out of the wind. Two of the crew were coiling ropes on the other side of the ship; rough-looking men with long beards, wearing faded jerkins. One of them was staring hard at me, with a heavy frown. I knew he was Jack, the ship's mate, as we had been introduced when we first came on board. I had been identified as Nathaniel, a serving lad, so as not to cause alarm by having a girl on board.

I was unsure why he was so concerned, but I put it from my mind and followed Robert down through the low doorway into the darkness below.

I could see a faint light ahead as we went down a few steps, then we came into a passageway that was lit by a small glass-covered tar lamp, swinging with the movement of the ship. Robert's face was a strange mix of black shadow and red skin in the lamp-light, and I had no doubt I looked much the same to him.

"We must check on your father," I said, my voice sounding unnaturally quiet after the shouting in the wind. "He did not look well just now."

Together we made our way to the cabin we had been allocated, and ducked through the low doorway. Inside we could see Sir John lying on the narrow cot in the light of a small lamp attached to the wall, his loud, regular snores clearly heard above the background creaking and groaning of the *Curliewe*'s timbers.

I sat on the floor with my back to the wall, and Robert did the same opposite me.

"Not only was he held in a dark dungeon these few days,

he did not sleep at all last night," I observed. "He has found welcome rest."

"Nor did you."

"I am less than half his age," I said. "I do not sleep so much."

There was a silence as we stared at each other. He seemed to be trying to find the right words to voice a concern on his mind. I stayed silent.

"I have been thinking," he said eventually. "Are we safe now? I am not sure we are."

Again I said nothing, waiting to see what was behind this thought.

"On Hythe Quay, when we dispatched that foul Sir Reginald and his men, did they not skulk off to the tavern, like beaten curs?"

"Aye, they did. And much in thanks to your action with that barrel."

He gave a small chuckle. "I would swear the man's nose was broken when I forced his helm down his face." Then he became serious again. "We thought they had accepted their fight was lost, and so would leave us in peace?"

"That is my dearest hope," I answered. But then I recalled Sir Reginald's ugly face, and his parting words; 'the next time we meet I will be better prepared, and you will not have a chance of escape...'

With a sudden sinking feeling in my stomach, I did not feel so free anymore. Robert's next words confirmed my fears.

"What if they did not skulk away like curs? What if they are even now, tracking us up the coast on horseback?"

"How so?" I asked. "They did not follow us to the boat. I made sure we were not observed when we boarded. So they would not have known which boat we are on, nor where we are bound." Then another thought struck me, "And the coast is low and flat. We can see for many leagues across it, and I can assure you, there have been no horsemen riding there."

"But what of the *Curliewe*?" he said. "There must be records kept of each boat that docks or departs. It would take only a few questions of the harbour master to confirm which one set sail shortly after the fight at the barrels, and where it is bound…" He looked at me with wide eyes, "We must assume that they asked such questions." He paused. "It is many hours faster to ride to Harwich inland than to sail round the coast from Maldon. So he will have had time to raise more men and ride directly. We must therefore assume that when we dock," he took a deep breath, "Sir Reginald will be on the quay to greet us."

We sat and stared at each other in silence as this awful information took root in each of our heads.

I could see the truth in what he said. Sir Reginald was no fool – he would never have simply walked away and left us in peace, especially after such a threat to my face. Indeed, it was I who was the fool; for having thought that once we were aboard the ship we were beyond pursuit.

It would be no trouble to enquire of the authorities at the quay as to the recent departures, and then to surmise that a boat going up the coast was likely to be giving us passage. The *Curliewe* was bound for Norwich with its cargo of wool, so Harwich was clearly a port it would put into on the way – and Harwich was at the mouth of the River Orwell, which led directly to Nacton and the home of Sir John Fitzwilliam…

"Then we must assume we will be met when we land," I said eventually. "We are like lambs being carried helpless to the slaughter." I ran my fingers through my hair. "I must think what we are to do," I said, but I got no further, as at that moment there was a sudden crash like canon fire, and the door to the little cabin was thrown open.

A man stood on the threshold, with others just visible behind him in the light of the room's single lamp. It was the ship's mate Jack, who had frowned at me so heavily up on the deck.

"There she be," he snarled, pointing at me, "the wench who would have us think she is a lad!"

He reached down and lifted me to my feet by the collar of my jerkin; as if I weighed no more than a mouse. "There she be!" he repeated. "'Tis a wench I tell you!"

Another man pushed past Jack and thrust his pock-marked face into mine. "Your name?" he demanded.

I wanted to say 'Nathaniel' – indeed, I knew my safety and that of Robert and Sir John, who was now awake and eying the proceedings sickly, depended on my carrying through this deception. But when it came to it, I knew that they could so readily expose the lie – one rip of my jerkin would reveal the truth for all the men to see – and I could not countenance that.

So I looked the man in the eye, raised my chin and said, "My name, sir, is Mary Fox."

"I knew it!" crowed Jack. "I heard it! I heard the man and the boy both call her 'Mary' upsides! The wind carried their words to me, clear as day. Not Nathaniel but Mary! I knew it was so!" Then his tone turned to menace. "So what is to do? We cannot be having a woman on board, or she will distract us from our duties and cause ill-luck." He turned to the others. "She must go overboard now! Not a moment more, or our luck will turn!"

At this Sir John raised his head. "You will do no such thing!"

Jack looked him up and down, with an expression on his face as if a worm had appeared on the cot. "I take no orders from a green-skinned landsman that cannot hold his spew," he said. "We take her to the rail!"

He grabbed me around the chest and lifted me bodily, so my feet were well clear of the floor. I kicked at his shins and yelled, "Put me down!"

"She has spirit, this one," he said, "but she takes her chance over the side!" Then he turned to carry me out of the cabin, pausing to duck his head as he approached the low lintel of the door.

As he did so, I felt him stagger forward, then heard a loud cracking sound as his forehead hit hard on the lintel. Immediately he dropped me, and I ran back into the cabin as he crunched down onto his knees, then toppled forward like an axed tree, with his feet in the air.

I rolled aside as Robert pushed the door shut onto the toes of Jack's boots, then slipped the bolt to secure it.

I stood up. "What did you do?" I yelled.

Robert nodded several times to himself, as if confirming that it was indeed he who had acted so decisively. "Yes, yes," he said. "I pushed him. I waited until he was bending for the door, and I pushed him. Yes. He hit his head. Hard. He hit it hard. I pushed him. Yes."

"Oh, Robert!" I said. "Thank you!"

"Well done, boy," added Sir John. "Well done!"

Robert looked at us both with wide eyes, as a furious banging and shouting started on the other side of the door. "But what do we do now?" he said.

"We wait," I replied. "Such a commotion will soon bring others. These men will not act with impunity when there are many more to witness their actions."

"You may be right, Mary," said Sir John, "but I fear the opposite effect." I could just make out the stern set of his face in the dim light. "I fear that they may be strengthened by their numbers, and dispose of you all the more easily."

"Would you have us break out, then?" I asked, "before such reinforcements arrive?"

"Nay." He paused a moment, as the banging increased. "There is no other option but to stay here until we make landfall. By then they will have seen that you bring no such ill luck." He slumped back down on the cot. "Or they will have taken an axe to the door and removed you by force," he added.

But his words had given me an idea.

Taking a deep breath, I pulled back the bolt. At this there was silence beyond.

I opened the door and immediately dropped to one knee, with my hands on my hips. I looked up, giving the steadiest stare into the ugly faces of Jake and his men that I could; for all that my stomach was churning and I was starting to feel as sick as Sir John had been on deck.

"Good sirs," I began.

"Hark!" said one. "The woman would talk."

"Good sirs," I repeated, as if the man had not spoken. "I have no wish to cause you ill luck, but only to have safe passage to Harwich." I dropped my gaze, then looked up again. "You may not have known me as a woman, but I could not conceal myself from the Fates. They have been fully aware of what I am, from the very moment I first stepped aboard the *Curliewe* many hours ago." I looked each man in turn. "Yet the ship still floats, does it not? The masts still stand proud? The luck of the ship still holds good?" I raised my chin and looked Jake in the eye. "Then why do you fear your luck will change, just because you now know the same as the Fates?"

"Because 'tis common knowledge that bad luck follows a wench on the seas," said Jack, rubbing his forehead, where a large red bruise was forming.

"But surely," I answered, "you presume that the Fates have malice in their hearts. Why did they not punish you for my presence earlier, even though you knew me not?"

"But now we do now," said Jack. "And now we know, I cannot stop my men from being distracted by you, and failing in their duties." He hawked and spat beside the door. "The crew of the *Ellyn* found a girl stowed away on board and the men's thoughts turned from their duties to the wench; then they all perished when an angry wind caught them ill-prepared. It pushed their ship over and sank her within minutes." He looked at the men around him as if seeking reassurance, and was met with knowing nods. "So we must rid the boat of your presence as quick as we can," he finished off. There were murmurings of assent, and the men started to come forward.

"Wait!" I said, holding up a hand, and they paused, their eyes glistening with menace in the half-light. "How long till we make landfall at Harwich?"

Jack said nothing, his black eyes fixed on mine.

"Two hours, maybe three at most," said a voice from behind him.

"Then I will make a bargain with you," I began.

But Jack growled, "You are not in a position to make such a thing."

"I will make a bargain," I repeated, "that works in your favour as much as mine."

There was a muttering at this, and I caught one of the exchanges between two men just behind Jack.

"The wench may have something to bargain with…"

"What does she have…?"

"I know what I would be having from her…" This was accompanied by a filthy snigger, that left me in no doubt what the man had in mind.

Without his eyes leaving mine, Jack held up his hand. I could see he had heard the exchange as well, and his burning stare confirmed that it only strengthened his case.

"Well?" he said when there was silence. "What is your bargain?"

I took a breath to steady my nerve. "You leave me and my companions in this cabin with the door locked, so I am out of sight and sound of your men. Then they can go about their duties without distraction. When we are a half hour's sail from Harwich, we are rowed ashore, so that your crew can then concentrate on docking the ship in the harbour without any further distraction."

My words echoed in the silence as Jake continued to stare into my eyes.

"And you will not have my drowning to weigh down your immortal soul," I added.

Jack seemed to come to a sudden conclusion. "Then let us go to it," he barked, and stepped away from the door. "Lock this door and bar it shut for good measure."

The door slammed and there was the sound of a key turning in the lock, then the sound of a heavy object being pushed hard up against it.

I looked from Robert to Sir John. Both were staring back at me with their mouths hanging open.

"You had the measure of a man twice your size and age," said Sir John. "T'was well done."

Robert said slowly, "T'was not just getting the better of the man that was well done." He put his hand on my arm. "It was the plan to have us rowed ashore before arriving at Harwich." He gave a dry chuckle, "and to slip into the town unseen by land, so avoiding the possibility of meeting de Courtney and his men at the harbour."

"That was my thought," I said, putting my hand over his. As I did so, a small shiver passed up my arm and I withdrew it quickly, as if I had placed it on a burning coal. "The shoreline is flat," I said, glancing at Robert, who looked as if he too had felt the shiver when our hands had touched. "So we can make landfall with ease, and good progress into Harwich on foot."

Robert and I parted, to sit once again with our backs to the wall. Sir John lay down on the cot once more, and was soon breathing deeply in time with the movement of the ship.

An uneasy silence fell between us. I could not get out

of my mind the unexpected feeling when our hands had touched, and, judging by his unwillingness to meet my eye, neither could Robert.

Eventually he looked up and said, "I fear I may have misjudged you, Mary Fox."

I considered my reply carefully. At the quay in Maldon he had promised we should work together, but perhaps he had not truly meant what he had said? Perhaps now this was changing, and he was starting to see me as a friend?

In truth, when I had misjudged him and called him 'Weed', had he also done the same to me? Had he given me a similar derogatory name in his mind? I glanced at him, and could see by his troubled look in return that this was almost certainly so.

I bit my lip. What could this name have been? He had called me 'the great Mary Fox' – with a fine sense of irony. So he must have seen me as someone who thought too much of herself; someone who would only act on another's behalf if they could achieve glory for themselves.

I drew a short breath and almost retched as a sick sensation came to my stomach. Was that how I seemed to others? An over-modest would-be heroine who only sought self-advancement?

Suddenly it all became clear.

He had seen me as a threat because I had found favour with his father, a favour that he himself could not achieve. In only four days I had gone from a total stranger to a sort of daughter to Sir John – and now I could see how this must have wounded his pride, and his manhood, to be displaced by such a girl.

Heaven knew what name he had given me! But sure enough it would have been as dismissive of me, as 'Weed' was of him.

"I am so sorry," I said.

I could see this surprised him. Whatever he expected me to say, it clearly was not that.

The ship rolled several times before he responded. "Why so?" he asked.

I glanced over at the cot, to check Sir John was still asleep. If the depth of his breathing was any indication, he was truly dead to the world.

"Because I never meant to come between you and your father."

There was another long silence. "No," he said eventually, "I know you meant well. I just took against you too easily." He leaned forward and took my hands in both of his. Once again I felt the sudden heat of his touch, but this time I did not pull away. "I assumed your wish was to be like another son to my father, when now I see you were just seeking his help, and offering your help in return." He rubbed his thumb gently against the back of my hand. "I thought you were un-natural; a girl who would be as Joan of Arc..." He hesitated, looking suddenly alarmed. "I... I... I thought you were forcing yourself on us as a leader, when my father should lead. But now I see you were simply seeing the best way forward and guiding us towards it."

I smiled inwardly. *Saint Joan* – as sure as night follows day, that had been his name for me.

"Robert," I said, "please believe me when I say I had no

wish to force my leadership on you. Indeed, I took my lead from you with the plan to be set ashore before Harwich. That was your doing, not mine."

"Yes, I had the thought," he answered, "but you acted on it. You seized the moment and made that black-eyed ruffian agree to have us set ashore."

"Well, it is for the best," I murmured, and gave him my most reassuring smile. "And in any case, the alternative was to be thrown over the side, and I cannot swim."

"I would have jumped in after you," he said.

"Oh!" I grinned. "You would have saved me?"

"Probably not," he said with a sheepish smile. "I cannot swim either."

13

CHAPTER THIRTEEN

The little jetty at Dovercourt was covered in slippery moss and mud, and I had to keep hold of Robert's sleeve as we clambered off the skiff that had brought us ashore.

I turned and looked back out to sea. The *Curliewe* seemed very small as she lay at anchor in the deeper waters, and the men aboard her were like black ants scurrying about her decks. I could not feel anything but relief to be on dry land once again, and away from the dangerous superstition of her crew. But at least she had brought us out of Maldon, and to this little village.

The oarsman who had rowed us silently ashore pushed away from the jetty and began his return to the ship, as I turned again to face the land.

"It is about a mile to the Harwich Quay," began Sir John.

"And I believe there are boats going up the River Orwell every week or so."

"We must stay hidden," said Robert, "until we can find such a boat."

"I have thought about that," I said, "and I agree we must be hidden. De Courtney and his men will be looking in the taverns and inns, and it is hard to keep concealed from a thorough search. And we will have to go to the quay to find and board a boat, so we run the risk of being spied there as well. We were spotted too easily in Maldon; we must not repeat the mistake." Then I nodded to myself as an idea I had been considering took final shape. "But I think there is a way we can be safe."

"Pray tell," said Sir John, who was now looking more rested and closer to his usual colour.

"They will be looking for an unkempt nobleman, his son and a girl in boy's garb, will they not?"

"Yes, I suppose they will."

"So, I say we avoid the taverns and inns, and stay in the finest hotel, as a husband and wife" – here I glanced at Robert, who blushed and looked away – "together with our manservant."

Sir John smiled broadly. "It sounds fun!" Then he frowned. "But where will you get the clothes and the money for a hotel?"

In answer I pulled out the strange leather purse with the Saxon design I had kept tied at all times inside the back of my breeches. "The coins you gave me from the brigand," I said. "There is still more than enough here for a gown and a hood for me, a fine new doublet and hose for Robert, and a plain servant's garb for you." I considered the unkempt beard he had grown since being taken prisoner and being held at Marchington Manor, "And a shave for you as well," I added. "Serving men are often beardless." With that I stepped off the landing stage onto the path that wound its way along the coast to the buildings of Harwich, just visible as a grey jagged line on the horizon. "Come," I said, looking back at Sir John and Robert, who had not moved, "we should find some-where to rest tonight, then make our way to Harwich in the morning."

The evening sun was sinking low in the western sky, as we found an inn at Dovercourt. It was a simple place, with a few rooms and a kitchen serving pie and ale, so we ate well before retiring for the night and sinking into a most welcome sleep.

The next morning dawned bright and sunny, and after breaking our fast with bread, cheese and small beer, we set off to walk into Harwich.

"First we must find the market," I observed over my shoulder to Robert and Sir John. "I trust there will be stalls selling clothes for us all."

I heard Sir John grunt acknowledgement as we walked on, but there was no such sound from Robert. I looked round, to see that he had stopped a few yards back and was standing stock still as if frozen to the spot. "What is it?" I asked.

"By chance they will have posted men in the market to seek us out?" he said, his voice sounding high, as though a rope was around his neck. "The *Curliewe* will have docked these many hours since, so they will have seen that we did not disembark – but a simple questioning of her crew will reveal that we were aboard." His eyes widened. "They will be combing the town for us, like a dog seeks the fox." He paused, as another, even worse thought appeared to hit him. "Perhaps they will kill me for the attack with the barrel in Maldon."

"Fie!" scolded Sir John. "I am sure they will do no such thing. And besides," he added, "they will be looking for the dirty fellow with grey hair who drank with old Tom Reeves these two nights past, not the fine young man in the well-cut doublet who will be escorting his noble-looking lady through the streets of Harwich."

"Unless they spy me before I can make good my change of style," said Robert, and I had to admit, he did have a point. He had not changed his clothes since we had first set out from the Blue Boar in the middle of the night before last, and was still wearing the black doublet and travel-worn cloak of the old soldier, Rob Godfrey. It was ideal clothing for the part of an ancient in the dark, but most odd for a young man in the daylight; not least because it was covered in dust and dirt and gave him the look of a vagrant. He would be identifiable with ease by any man who had been at the quay in Maldon, as well as by any man told to look for just a such a fellow.

More than that, I suspected that Sir Reginald's men would be told to look particularly for the strange group we presented: a dusty young man, an unkempt older man and a small girlish boy.

But if it was easy to identify us as a group of three, maybe we could change that?

"I suggest we each travel alone into Harwich," I said, "and

keep to side streets with our heads held low. They will be looking for us all together; by splitting up, we will confuse their search." I paused. "And perhaps you could lose the distinctive old cloak that marks you out so?"

So it was that we split up on the outskirts of the town, with agreement that we would each approach the market from a different street, and keep apart once we were there.

I made my way to the market with my head down, keeping well to the side of each street to avoid the stinking channel of filth that ran down the middle. I slipped into a shadowed doorway as I entered the market square, to observe without being seen myself.

I was hit by the colour and noise of hundreds of people thronging around the stalls; gaily dressed men in bright doublets and feathered caps; women in flowing gowns, some with hoods in the new French style of Queen Anne Boleyn but most with simple cotton coifs; small children playing with wooden marionettes; stallholders shouting their wares and arguing the price with their customers; live sheep, pigs and goats adding their noise to the hubbub...

But I forced myself not to be distracted by these many little stories of everyday life; instead, I looked carefully around for the men who might be in the service of Sir Reginald.

The man leaning against the door of a butcher's shop? He had the look of a soldier, and was gazing about most observantly. Or the fellow by the tavern, his feathered cap pushed down so his eyes could not be seen – was he keeping watch over that side of the market?

I slid further into the shadows as I watched these men.

After a moment the man by the tavern raised his head and

stared hard into the crowd. I followed his gaze, dreading to see that he had spotted either Robert or Sir John, but could see only a group of women walking in his direction. One of them went up to him and held out a basket of purchases. He took it with a warm smile, and together they started to walk away.

I laughed at this little show of married contentment – then I frowned to myself. It really was too bad I could not share such happiness while my stepfather still conspired to sell me off to Sir Reginald like a parcel of meat, much as the ones that were being traded all round the market.

But if not Sir Reginald, then who should I marry?

Robert?

I gasped at the thought. Truly?

Could I become Mistress Mary Fitzwilliam, were he to ask? The contented wife that he envisioned back in the forest? He had expressed his wish to be a fine gentleman, 'possessed of a good wife and many children'. Would I want to be the wife that was 'possessed,' turning out children for him, like a caged hen laying daily eggs?

I shook my head and stamped my foot on the cobbled stones. No! I should not hold such a jaded view of marriage! The purpose of a woman is to be a wife and mother; that is God's law! Who was I to defy God in this? I should welcome the chance to cleave myself to a good man, and become an upstanding wife, attending church with my husband and children every holy day and keeping a fine house to make him proud...

I looked across the market, but it was not the worthy people of Harwich that I saw. Instead, I saw myself in my best gown, my hair scraped back and concealed under a French hood, gathering my children to my side, while my husband – an older, fatter version of Robert – laughed at the antics of our youngest daughter and chivvied his oldest boy to don his hat so the Fitzwilliam family could step out and make their way to the church to hear mass being said by Father Whoever...

Aye, that should be my wish for a happy and contented life – Mistress Fitzwilliam, wife and mother.

So why did this picture of married contentment make my stomach feel as if it was full of lead? As if part of me had died inside?

The man by the tavern suddenly pushed his feathered cap back and looked up.

My heart quickened as I studied him – now I could see his face, I could not miss the red wheal across the bridge of his nose. It was the man that Robert had struck with the barrel on Hythe Quay!

I followed his stare across the market. What – or more particularly, who – had captured his attention?

The man sprang away from the tavern, and started to push purposefully through the crowd.

The leaden feeling in my stomach miraculously disappeared as I took up the chase. Slipping out of the shadows, I walked quickly across to where he had been standing. Keeping a few feet back, I followed him across the market, my head down.

He was so fixed on whatever he was chasing that he seemed unaware I was keeping close behind him. I searched the crowds ahead to see if I could identify his quarry, and then almost froze to the spot. A thin man in black with dusty hair was standing by a stall, leaning in to talk to the seller.

It was Robert.

I looked back at Sir Reginald's man, closing in fast on Robert, who seemed oblivious to the danger. If the man could not quickly be stopped, it would be disaster.

He strode past a stall selling bread, and I noted that the baker was a burly fellow with a red face and a smooth, hairless head. He, and a small mousy woman I assumed to be his wife, were serving customers with loaves from a stack on a table behind them.

This gave me an idea.

A moment after Sir Reginald's man had gone past, I ran up to the baker. He was busy attending to a woman in a grey woollen gown, but a quick pluck at his sleeve caught his attention.

"Please sir," I said, "that man has taken a loaf of bread from your stall!"

"What is that, boy?" he answered, looking down at me with a frown.

"That man with the feathered cap!" I pointed to where the feathers could be seen waving as the man moved through the crowd. "I saw him take a loaf as he passed your stall!"

"By thunder!" shouted the baker. "Another cursed thief! Mind the stall, Winnie!"

With that, he set off after Sir Reginald's man, parting the crowd with shouts of "Out my way!" as he came up behind his quarry.

I scampered off to a safe distance to watch. He caught up with the man just yards before the clothier's stall, pulling him round and shouting angrily. The response was as could be expected; Sir Reginald's man showed surprised innocence, and it was clear that the matter would soon be sorted. Fortunately, the altercation caught the attention of all around, including Robert, who visibly paled as he saw the man's face. He quickly settled his transaction and set off in the opposite direction.

Still keeping my head down, I ran after Robert, watching him from a short distance as he made his way out of the market clutching his new clothes. Once I was reasonably certain he was clear away, I turned and pushed my way back into the crowds. There was a shop selling fine women's things on the far side of the square. As I made my way towards it, I made sure to keep well clear of the baker's stall.

It was a very different Mary Fox that stepped out of this shop an hour or so later.

The lady that made her dignified progress across the market square and headed towards the Three Cups Hotel bore no resemblance to the grubby boy who had entered it earlier in the day. From the beaded black French hood covering her head and the yellow gown with embroidered sleeves, to the dainty slippers on her feet, she was every inch the noblewoman.

And most uncomfortable, too.

Now I recalled why I hated to wear such clothes, much to my stepfather's disgust. Scarcely a day had passed back in Marchington Manor, but he had complained loudly that it was not natural for a girl to wear breeches and a jerkin, and forgo the many gowns that he had so thoughtfully provided. I would point out that there was no joy in being so constricted that breathing was a luxury, or being able to walk no faster than a snail so as not to trip over voluminous skirts, but this held no sway with Sir Andrew. "Why," he would ask, "am I burdened with such an ungodly girl, who would defy me, and dress as if she were a man?"

"I am not ungodly," I answered on one such occasion when we were seated in the Great Hall at family supper. "I attend mass as prescribed by law."

"Aye," he replied, his knife paused halfway to his mouth with a piece of venison speared on the tip, "but not, I would wager, by choice. And anyhow," he added, taking the meat and chewing as he talked, "wearing either a boy's garb, or a plain dress like a serving girl, is not seemly in a woman of your position." He stared at me with his brow furrowed. "It is a disgrace to the memory of the sainted mother you dispatched so thoughtlessly." I let this pass; to comment would be as fruitless as ever. "And besides," he continued, "I can scarce hold up my head in the county, for I know as a fact, that they say Sir Andrew Fox cannot control his daughter."

"They should better remark on how Mary Fox thinks for herself," I answered.

Suddenly he stabbed his knife deep into the wooden trencher in front of him – a violent gesture that killed all conversation from the others in the room in an instant.

"God's wounds!" he snarled, glaring at me over the still quivering handle. "You make a mockery of me, young lady?"

"Nay," I answered slowly, "I merely point out that they should recognise a person who is able to think for themselves, and act accordingly. That should be a cause for celebration, whether it is a girl or a boy."

There was a hushed silence from the rest of the family as they waited on Sir Andrew's response. He held his tongue a few moments, seeming to consider his options. Then he took a careful breath and said in a more measured tone, "Mary, you are not free to think for yourself. You are a woman, and a woman is, by law, subject to her father's, then to her husband's will." He worked his knife free, then held it up before my face. "I trust I make myself clear?"

I lifted my chin and stared back. "Perfectly clear, Father."

"Good." He jabbed another piece of meat and stuffed it in his mouth. "Then I do not want to have this conversation again."

But, of course we did, I thought, as I made my stately way up to the door of the hotel. Many times we had repeated it, right up to the day when I had had enough and had set out on my adventure in the forest; the one that had brought me to Harwich and this cursed yellow gown.

I twisted slightly in the tight bodice to try and allow even a small breath, and stepped inside.

The Three Cups consisted of a well-appointed tavern on the ground floor, with wood panelled walls decorated with the severed heads of several stags and foxes, looking across the room at each other with dull eyes. Between them were a couple of heavy tapestries decorated with hunting scenes, almost as if these were the occasions when the stags and foxes had met their unfortunate fates. A stair led upwards from one side of the room, no doubt to the bedrooms.

"How can I assist you, mistress?"

A small man with a long beard and no hair on his head was approaching, his eyebrow raised in query.

"I seek my husband, sir," I answered. "His name is Robert Godfrey."

"Aye, Mistress Godfrey, your husband is already arrived and has taken a room with his manservant. You may find them in the first room to the right at the top of the stairs."

"Thank you," I said, and made my way up.

Sir John answered almost immediately I finished the secretly agreed knock, and I gasped as I took in his manner and garb. He was no longer the assured nobleman, but was beardless and wearing the drabbest of garments. His hat was plain and black, as were his tunic and breeches.

"By heaven," I exclaimed, "you are unrecognisable!"

"It is not I," he said with a wink and a smile, "for Robert – your supposed husband – is far more changed than I."

He stood back and I went in.

Robert was standing by the fire – and when I saw him, I gasped in amazement.

He was every inch the nobleman. His blue doublet was fastened from his waist to his throat with silver buttons, with a small lace collar rising up to his chin. Pale cream sleeves billowed from his shoulders, which were made broader and more manly by a wide, black overgown. His legs were in fine gartered black hose and the whole ensemble was finished off with a pair of black leather shoes.

I realised I must have been smiling as I took in the new Robert, for he smiled at me also, and I suspected he had been making the same appraisal of me as I had of him.

"Pray turn and let me see you all round," he asked, confirming my thought.

I turned left then right, looking coquettishly back over my shoulder, then dropped into a low curtsy.

"I realise I am now seeing the genuine Mary Fox," he said, stepping forward and lifting me gently by the chin, "and her beauty truly takes my breath."

"Nay," I replied, looking into his eyes, "this is the Mary Fox that my stepfather so desires, but it is not me." I looked away. "The Mary Fox you have known these past days is the real one, not this constricted creature."

The smile disappeared from his face, and I cursed myself for being so truthful. Then he rallied, and said, "So I must enjoy her while I have her, here in Harwich."

"Until we can get a boat up the Orwell to Nacton," said Sir John. "Which I have confirmed will be in three days."

"Then we have three days to maintain our disguises," I observed, "and ensure we do not come to the attention of de Courtney or his men."

14

CHAPTER FOURTEEN

Anyone observing the stairway into the main tavern later that evening would have seen the tall, well-appointed Master Robert Godfrey and his elegant wife Mary stepping down hand-in-hand, then being shown by the innkeeper to a small table in a secluded area in a corner of the room.

The observer would have noted how Master Godfrey solicitously pulled back the chair for his wife, before helping her to sit and arranging her yellow gown, almost as if she did not know how to do this simple task for herself…

…But thankfully, no-one appeared to be observing.

I thanked Robert for his small act of kindness with a smile. He bowed in response, before adjusting his shiny new sword belt, sitting down and passing me a small poignard knife, ready for the meal.

The table gave us an excellent view of the many people taking their supper; the sailors, the local yeomen, the ladies of dubious standing, and a few of a more elevated class, such as some men who appeared to be merchants, huddled together and presumably conducting business, or a group of younger men with well-cut clothes who were getting progressively more drunk and ever louder in their boisterous camaraderie.

"You were right, Mary," said Robert, glancing at this group with a critical eye, "though we are in plain sight here, in truth we are well-hidden." He flinched as one of the young men slammed his tankard down with a thump that would waken the dead, accompanied by roars of laughter from his fellows as his ale splashed across the table. "Any pursuer would be much taken by the colour and noise of the rest of the room before seeing
us in the corner."

I leaned forward. "I agree, but that does not allow us to drop our guard." I took his hand in mine, choosing to ignore the red flush that appeared immediately from under his lace collar. "We cannot assume they will fail to recognise us, for all that we bear very little resemblance to the ragged pair that fought them on the dock at Maldon yesterday morning."

I made to remove my hand, and he quickly placed his other across it.

"Nay, Mary," he said, his cheeks now turning crimson, "let us continue the act of being a loving husband and wife." His thumb stroked gently across the back of my hand. "It does please me greatly."

"But it is an act, nonetheless," I said.

His face fell, but his hand stayed where it was, and the stroking continued. "I must apologise," he said. "I fear I upset you earlier, with my talk of the real Mary Fox."

"Not at all," I answered, then paused, waiting for his cheeks to begin their return to a more normal colour. "I am flattered that you think me a beauty…"

"I do, Mary," he interrupted.

"…but I must once again stress that this…" I gestured down at the bodice that made such a prisoner of my chest, "…this is not how I chose to present myself." I shook my head slightly. "The real Mary Fox prefers to run free than to be so constricted."

"You would have been better born a boy," he observed.

"Aye," I answered, "it would have been more apt." And it would have perhaps softened my stepfather's cold heart to have had another man in the family, not a wayward girl.

"But," he began, then stopped, biting on his lip and looking most unsure, almost as if Weed had once again returned from the forest.

"Go on," I prompted.

"But Mary," he drew a breath, and his thumb stilled. "But, Mary, why? Why do you want to run free?" His brow furrowed so deeply I thought it would push his eyes closed. "Why? You have been born into a good family, with wealth enough to buy you the finest clothes and a rare beauty to match them – why do you not value this as all other girls do?"

I thought of his sister; ailing at home while the Broken Sword was missing, but no doubt a pretty young girl, normally keen to look her best and wear the finest gowns for her mother. What did Robert know of a girl brought up without such a mother; indeed without any female in her life other than a dried-up old nurse, because her stepfather refused to re-marry? A girl constantly reminded that her dead mother was the embodiment of female perfection, and that it was the girl's own fault that this ideal woman had died? A girl who was forced to watch as a procession of simpering women, each wearing the latest fashionable gown and with their faces ever more garishly painted, passed through her stepfather's rooms, leaving her to think that such women were quite worthless, and wishing never to become like them?

Was it any wonder, I thought as I held his enquiring gaze, that such a girl would value the privileges enjoyed by her brothers and wish to run as free as them, away from the stifling constriction of society's expectations?

True, I was not rendered sick by a centuries-old curse like his sister. But there was a curse that I too was suffering under, and it was a curse called Sir Reginald de Courtney, who would damn me for the rest of my life if I were to become his unfortunate wife. And then there was the curse of my stepfather, ready to do me to death if he got his hands on me and I refused to marry.

I wanted to explain all this to Robert, to help him understand why I behaved as I did, but I knew he would not see past the standard image of womanhood that the law, society, and indeed God, demanded. His sister and his mother gave him a different viewpoint, and I knew he could never see me the way I saw myself.

"Robert," I said, "there are reasons, believe me. But you have to understand, they are my reasons, not yours." I paused. "I am the way I am, and any man who wants to win my affections has to accept me for that person. Not," I added, "the person they would have me be."

"I see." He let go of my hand, his eyes flicking across mine. "You are a good person, Mary Fox," he said after a while, "a very good person. You are helping my father and me to get the Broken Sword back to our family, which, God willing, shall restore our womenfolk, and our fortunes, to health. You have no obligation to do this, but you are doing it, and we are grateful." He took a breath. "And you put up with my cowardly behaviour…" I shook my head. "…no, hear me out," he continued. "You put up with my cowardly, ungrateful behaviour, and what is more, you went out of your way to help me understand how I should become a better person. I have much to thank you for, Mistress Mary Fox." He paused, clearly deciding what else to say, and I let him have the silence he needed. "We are close to Nacton, and, by the grace of God, we shall soon have the Broken Sword back in its rightful place. With our fortunes then restored, the Fitzwilliams of Nacton will once again be a prominent family…" I took a small breath – I could see where this might be leading "…so, Mary, I would offer you the chance to become part of that family – one that will love you and honour you for who you are."

He paused, then swallowed hard and said, "Mistress Mary Fox, I would you do me the great honour of becoming my wife."

I stared at Robert, as he gazed back with a hopeful smile. What could I tell him? That I had considered him as a possible husband, and it made me feel sick to my stomach? That becoming the contented wife of a country landowner and mother to his children may be the thing that society expects, but would not be for me? That Mary Fox could never be tied down?

But then…

Would this mean I should have to 'run free' for all my days? Would I never experience the warm love of a husband and children? Was I committing myself to the life of an itinerant adventuress, forever moving from one parish to the next and never settling down to the acceptance of a community?

This earnest young man was giving me a way to find some form of love and acceptance – and knowing as he did so, that I would be an unconventional wife. So should I take his offer and become betrothed? He was holding out the chance for me to be loved and honoured for myself, and not as the ideal wife… which would mean he would have to be an un-conventional husband and accept I would not play the part of the comely wife and dress as society would see fit…

Maybe, if he was prepared to do this, then the match would work for both of us…

"Robert," I said slowly, "I am deeply honoured by your offer, but I cannot answer you now." I took his hand in both of mine. "I need some time to think on this most deeply."

He pursed his lips and nodded. "I know," he said, "I under-stand this would be a change in your plans, and that we have known each other less than a week. But please know this, Mary, as I have become acquainted with you these past few days, I have grown to love you, and can think of no greater happiness than to share the rest of my life with you."

"Then let me think on it," I repeated. "I will answer when I am ready, and give you my reasons."

He started to answer, but we were interrupted by the arrival of a young girl with a tray containing a steaming pie and two tankards.

"Gammon pie and ale," she announced, setting the tray down.

"Thank you," I responded. I turned to Robert once she had gone. "You were about to say?"

"Only that I will wait for your answer, and hope it is favourable," he said, then added, "but I would not wait to eat this pie, for I am quite starving."

---0---

After we had finished the pie in companionable silence and our tray had been collected, I sat back to allow some air into my chest.

"I feel all the better for that," I said. "But now we should get back to your father upstairs, and not linger in sight of these people a moment more than we have to."

He nodded, and we were about to stand when I noticed that one of the merchants who had been huddled at the table nearby, was now staring hard at Robert.

My breath caught in my throat, as he stood up and strode purposefully over to our table.

"Robert Fitzwilliam?" he asked. "Son of Sir John? I thought I recognised you."

I wanted to deny it; to say the man was mistaken, and that our names were Robert and Mary Godfrey, but I could see Robert had been caught off guard, and had made the smallest nod of recognition.

"Master Geoffrey Simmonds," he said. "You have bought wool from the farms owned by my father."

"Aye, and good prices they fetched, too, young Fitzwilliam," answered Simmonds, a little too loudly for my comfort. Then his face fell and he assumed a more sombre expression. "I was distressed to hear your father's lands were enclosed, and extraordinary rents due." Robert nodded and Simmonds continued, his face even more sombre. "And also that your mother and sister have been unwell. I trust they are now recovered?"

"I know not," answered Robert. "My father and I have been away nigh on three weeks, seeking a... a cure. But we shall be returning very shortly."

Then he turned to me and looked me up and down a moment. "And you are returning with a charming bride, I see," he said, sweeping off his hat and bowing low. "I am honoured to make your acquaintance, Mistress Fitzwilliam."

"Master Simmonds," I replied, bowing my head, "Mary... er... Fitzwilliam. I am honoured to meet you."

I caught Robert's eye and shook my head slightly, to warn him not to reveal any more truths. He gave a small nod in return, although I feel there was perhaps also a look of quiet triumph, for he had gone from proposal to seeming marriage in but a few minutes.

Fortunately Geoffrey was putting his hat back on, and did not spot this little exchange.

"You are a lucky man, Robert, to have a bride so fair."

"Thank you, Master Simmonds. I am indeed very fortunate."

I turned away, to hide my smile.

"Geoffrey, please. Call me Geoffrey. I have known your father too many years to be so formal."

"For sure… Geoffrey."

"That is better. Now tell me," Geoffrey said, "are you both staying here in the Three Cups?"

"We are, as we await a boat up the Orwell."

"Well, I believe the next boat sails in three or four days." Geoffrey put his hand on Robert's shoulder. "In the meantime, I insist you and your lovely wife come home with me and become my honoured guests."

I could see Robert was unsure how to respond, so I said, "That is most kind Master Simmonds." I gave him my most demure smile from beneath lowered lashes. "Are you sure that would not be an imposition?"

This seemed to have the desired effect. "Not at all. Mistress Simmonds and I would be delighted."

I caught Robert's eye again, and gave him the slightest nod, wanting him to see that this would be an ideal way to keep out of sight until we could sail.

"Then that is settled." He turned to Robert and they started to converse quietly, no doubt about the price of wool, or somesuch.

My attention was caught by the main door opening, and I glanced idly over the room to see what manner of person might be entering.

It was a thin older man, his hat pulled low over his lined face.

I swear the blood ran cold in my veins. I recognised the frame, and the beard…

It was Sir Reginald.

He stopped as he entered, and swept the room with his dark eyes. Immediately I turned away, pulling Robert round so our backs were to the door.

"Eh? What ails?" exclaimed Robert. Then he froze at the look on my face. "Is it – that, that man?"

I nodded, not trusting myself to speak.

Geoffrey Simmonds frowned, looking from Robert to me and back again. "There is a well-dressed older man who has entered," he said, thankfully quiet this time. He glanced across Robert's shoulder. "He searches the room. Does this man concern you?" I nodded again. "Why so?"

"He is looking for us," I whispered.

Geoffrey again glanced across at Sir Reginald. "He has a face like thunder. I like him not."

"Nor I. Nor Mary," breathed Robert.

"Why does he search for you?"

"Ahh," I said, playing for time, as I looked to Robert for inspiration. The truth would not serve. I had not denied Geoffrey's assumption that I was Robert's wife, so I could hardly explain that Sir Reginald sought me to marry me… but then I had a moment of clarity and smiled grimly. "He is in league with my father, who disapproves of Robert."

"A love match, eh?" Geoffrey grinned like a co-conspirator. Then he became serious again. "So your father would cast you apart from each other?"

"He would," I said. "We must not be seen by this man."

Geoffrey glanced again across the room. "He looks towards us, but there is no recognition."

I kept my back squarely to the door, silently asking God in His infinite wisdom and kindness to please, please, please send Sir Reginald away…

"Oh," Geoffrey's eyes widened. "He comes towards us."

I stiffened, as the hated voice came from just behind my shoulder.

"Good sir, I beg your pardon, and that of your companions, but I wonder if you have seen a young couple we seek? The man is dressed in black and has much dirt in his hair, and the girl is to be seen in the garb of a boy."

Geoffrey shook his head slowly. "Nay, good sir," he answered, "they sound a most singular couple. I would recall them, most assuredly. But no, I do not."

"You are sure?" There was a pause, and no sound of movement behind me, save for the slight creak of a leather sword belt as Sir Reginald must have shifted his weight. "The man is tall, much as your companion here with his back to me, and the girl is of similar stature to this lady here…"

"Again, sir, I must say, I do not know of this couple," Geoffrey repeated.

There was another pause, and again I offered prayers to make Sir Reginald accept what he was told and leave.

Again, I was ignored, and there was no movement behind me.

Then I almost cried out, as I felt his hand on my shoulder.

"Perhaps I should enquire of this good lady?" Sir Reginald said, as he pulled me round to face him, almost retching in my fear. "This fine lady who flinches at my touch…" He smiled, a sick, twisted grimace. "This lady who dresses at last as befits her station… Mary Fox!"

I took a deep, careful breath, then forced myself to keep the fear out of my face.

"Mary Fox, sir?" I raised an artful eyebrow. "I know of no Mary Fox. My name is Mistress Godfrey." I managed a cold smile. "I fear you have mistaken me for someone else, sir."

I could see Sir Reginald was unnerved for a moment, then he recovered his confidence.

"Nay, you do not fool me. Stop this nonsense and come quietly, or it will be the worse for you."

But he had been slightly unsure that I was Mary Fox, so I decided to try and use this to press my advantage.

"Do not touch me, sir," I demanded, moving my shoulder so his hand fell away, "I repeat, you have me confused with someone else."

He smiled; a nasty, sneering grimace. "Come now, Mary…"

Out of the corner of my eye I saw Robert start to reach for the sword at his belt.

"You said that the woman you seek dresses as a boy," I said. "Do I look like such a one?"

Sir Reginald was silent, as he eyed my gown. Then he said, "Clothes can be changed."

"And the man has dirty hair and is dressed in black…" I put my hand over Robert's, preventing it going further towards the hilt of his sword. The last thing I wanted was for him to make any foolish move.

"As I say, clothes can be changed."

"And mistakes can be made, sir," I said, keeping my voice level. "As you have done, confusing me with this other woman. This… Mary Fox, was it?"

Sir Reginald's face started to flush, and he started to draw his own sword. "I said, come now, Mary, and we shall not have cause for regret." He gripped his hilt and drew it slightly more.

"Do you threaten me, sir?" I asked, putting an edge of justified outrage into my voice. "Do you draw your sword on a woman? I have said I am not the person you seek."

Geoffrey stepped forward. "You heard Mistress Godfrey, sir." He started to draw his own sword. "She says she is not this Mary Fox, so I suggest you accept that she speaks the truth, and leave us in peace."

Sir Reginald looked from Geoffrey to Robert to me but said nothing, although his face grew more flushed.

"I repeat," said Geoffrey, "leave us in peace." He drew his sword a little further. "Or I will drive you hence on the edge of my blade."

Just then there was a shout from behind Sir Reginald. It was one of the rowdy young men from the nearby table, a small, slight fellow with flowing hair. He staggered unsteadily towards us. "I say, mistress" he yelled to me, "is this man bothering you?" He pulled Sir Reginald round, then looked at me with eyes that seemed to be having difficulty focusing. "Was he threatening you, mistress?"

Then he noticed Geoffrey. "Master Geoffrey Shimmonds… Summons… Simmonds!" He bowed and swept off his cap.

"Master Tobias Whyte," Geoffrey returned, bowing also. "I saw you not, earlier."

"No masher… matter," responded the young man. "You are well met, Master Simmonds." He turned back. "Now, is this fellow threatening you?" he repeated to me.

Sir Reginald snapped at him, "Away, small man, this is no concern of yours."

"I should think it is, by the Lord!" answered Master Whyte. "I have been watching, and if I see an old stick like you threatening a fine young lady, I make it my business!"

"You are drunk, sir," snarled Sir Reginald, towering over the young man. "Now be gone, before you fall over, or I fell you with my sword."

"Are you threatening me now?" asked Tobias. "Are you, by God? Are you threatening me?" He started fumbling for his sword.

"I said be gone!" barked Sir Reginald, and the young man stopped still.

"What is it you say?"

"Be gone!"

Tobias looked him up and down, his eyes now seeming to focus more clearly. "Listen, you dried up old fart…"

Just then a couple of his drinking companions joined the group.

"What passes, Tobias?" asked one loudly. "Is this man giving you trouble?"

"Aye," said Tobias. "He accuses this fine lady here of being a fox or somesuch, which she denies, and he will not leave her alone."

"We cannot be having such ungallant behaviour," said the second man, then he bowed to me. "Is this man bothering you, mistress?"

Sensing my opportunity, I smiled at the second man. "He has me mistaken for some other lady he seeks, sir," I said, making my eyes as wide as possible. "He says this lady pretends to be a boy – whereas as you can see…" I stood back slightly, to give him the full view of my gown, "I do nothing of the sort."

He ran his eyes up and down me, coming to rest on my heaving chest.

"Nay, that is for sure." Then he faced Sir Reginald.

"You, sir, are ungracious and ill-benefitting the rank that you seem to belong to."

"I have no interest in your ill-informed opinions, boy," responded the older man. "Now I suggest you and your ineffectual drunken companions get back to your places and leave us alone. This is no concern of yours." He turned to me. "Come now, Mary, and we shall say no more of this."

"Do you present your back to me?" demanded Tobias. He pulled Sir Reginald round by the sleeve.

Then suddenly Sir Reginald's sword was out and the tip pushed up against Tobias's breast.

"I will not tell you again, boy," snarled Sir Reginald. "Be gone!"

As Tobias backed away, his two companions circled round Sir Reginald, their swords also drawn. At this, their other companions appeared, adding their swords to the group that now completely encircled the older man.

"Now what do you say?" asked one of them with a triumphant smile.

"I say you are all drunk, and this is assault," said Sir Reginald calmly.

"It is not yet," said Tobias's original friend. "But it will be if you do not desist." He put his own point to Sir Reginald's shoulder, as his other companions all moved closer and found other places on Sir Reginald's person to rest their points.

I nodded to Robert and Geoffrey, and could see we were all of the same mind.

As Sir Reginald looked in turn at each of the men in front of him, and no doubt felt the presence of those behind, we three slipped quietly away from the group and made our exit, leaving Sir Reginald to find his own way out of the situation.

15

CHAPTER FIFTEEN

"You really are most kind, Geoffrey," said Sir John, leaning back in his chair and studying the deep red claret swirling around in his glass. "My son and I, and our beloved Mary, thank you for making us your guests and shielding us from those who would split us up."

It was an hour later, and we were happily installed in Geoffrey's well-appointed Harwich town house, enjoying some fine wine as we sat by the fire in his comfortable parlour, surrounded by impressive oak-panelling and overlooked by the stern faces of his family from their framed paintings.

"I do not mind saying," observed Geoffrey, "that the man who was searching for you seemed most objectionable."
He paused as a young servant entered with another flagon of wine. "Thank you, Daniel," he said, as the boy bowed and withdrew. "I understand well that you needed to construct a disguise." He refilled his glass and raised it to Sir John. "How

did you maintain the garb and demeanour of a lowly servant? Most remarkable!"

"T'was no hardship, my dear fellow," Sir John replied. "It was all the work of young Mary here. She came up with the plan, and we did but follow it through."

"And this is all to get back to your home without Mary being separated from her new husband?"

I caught Sir John's eye and shook my head a fraction to warn him off any comment on this falsehood.

"Indeed," he said.

Geoffrey gave a small, hollow chuckle. "That man sent by her father was surrounded by hostile young drunkards, armed with swords and not best disposed to him, when we slipped away."

"A situation he brought upon himself," observed Robert.

"In my experience, such bullies are often arrant cowards when faced down by those stronger than themselves."

I spoke up at this. "Sir Reginald is a bully, that is for certain." I paused. "But do not dismiss him as a coward. I would not have him marked for that."

Geoffrey regarded me over the rim of his glass. "Then he is more the fool, I say. Those young men would fold in the face of submission, for there would be no sport in it." He thought a moment. "But in the face of an aggressive adversary, I warrant they would return that aggression tenfold."

"If so," Sir John suggested, "then I would not give a fig for the man's chances."

"I wish I had your confidence," I said. "For I fully expect Sir Reginald to have found a way out of the situation we left him in." I took a sip of my wine, drawing comfort from its rich, deep warmth, as I imagined how the scene would have played out after we had left. "While I would welcome the thought that Tobias and his friends would have had Sir Reginald dancing on the points of their swords, my guess is that he would have changed from the aggressor to their charming drinking companion in but a half hour."

No doubt he would have persuaded them that he was just a kindly gentleman, more sinned against than sinning, in pursuit of the wayward maiden he truly loved (that would be me). I could see them even now, first listening to his impassioned speech, accepting that they had gravely misjudged him and he was indeed the victim of the situation, then finally raising a toast to their new-found companion and vowing to help him win back the hand of the fair maid. Indeed, for all he had a foul temper and unnatural desires, I knew he was capable of persuading others to his cause.

I recalled the occasion when Francis and I were young children, and we were dining in the Great Hall at Sir Reginald's magnificent house in Essex. In the middle of the banquet, a group of tenant farmers tried to gain access with some grievance or other. Their numbers had made them bold, and they were outside the house demanding to be heard. Sir Reginald's men had made to send them away, but the man himself, on hearing of their grievance, instead invited them into the hall.

I still recall these ragged fellows, some thirty or so, being marched into the hall and assembled in front of the high table where Sir Reginald, my stepfather and other local dignitaries were sitting. I watched them as they stared around the room, their heads bare, twisting their caps in their hands as they took in the well-dressed nobles, fine furnishings and intricate tapestries.

My stepfather looked as if he would have them all hung for insubordination, but Sir Reginald called their leader up to the table.

"What is your grievance?" he asked.

The man listed a set of problems that I do not now recall, except there was something about lands and farming. He was clearly angry, and would only have to say the word and the men with him could become destructive. I do remember being frightened, and holding Francis's hand under the table, and being reassured when he gripped it tightly.

Sir Reginald listened intently, letting the man finish. When he was silent, Sir Reginald said, "I do understand, Ned. It is hard for you to manage. Here is what we will do..." Then he set out some conditions that sounded most reasonable, and seemed to pacify the man Ned, so that he smiled, thanked Sir Reginald and took his men away in peace.

"I do not believe he conceded anything," whispered Francis to me as the normal hubbub returned. "Yet he has them believing he has given them all they sought. T'was well done indeed."

I stared into my wine a moment as I forced my thoughts back into the present time, then looked up at Geoffrey, Robert and Sir John. "For all I know him to be a monster, he has the capacity for understanding others," I said, "and can be a sympathetic person if necessary. I believe we must assume that not only has he remained untouched by those boys, but has most likely now become their leader."

"That would be quite a turnaround," observed Sir John.

"I agree," I said, "and for all that he would have gained the trust of those boys with a nod, a wink and a winning smile, I do not underestimate how angry he will be with us, for slipping away and leaving him so." I bit my lip as a thought occurred to me. "And with me, for telling such a brazen lie to his face." I looked at Robert. "I trust God will forgive me for the sin of lying."

"I am sure He will," said Geoffrey before Robert could answer. "For it was done from the purest of motives."

I smiled and nodded, but offered up a silent prayer anyway.

"I am sure Mary is right," said Sir John. "So we need to stay a step ahead if we are to get back to Nacton."

"And return to your womenfolk, in order to nurse them back to health?" asked Geoffrey. There was a slight edge to his voice, as if this was a leading question.

"That is my overriding aim," Sir John answered.

Geoffrey paused. "I have known you many years, and although our relationship is based on trade, I believe we are friends?" Sir John nodded slowly. "Then, as your friend, I must ask you this." He cleared his throat. "I must ask how you have left your sick wife and daughter these many weeks, when you could have been caring for them in their illness?"

There was a cold silence that lasted an uncomfortably long time.

"Forgive me, I have gone too far," Geoffrey said eventually, his face losing much of its colour.

Sir John shook his head. "Nay, good fellow, it is a fair question, and one I should most definitely answer, as to a friend." He drew a breath and appeared to study his shoes with the greatest interest. "First, I must say that their illness is more of a general malaise that renders them listless and without appetite or energy. So while I would have deep concern for their health if we were to stay away for much longer, I knew that they would be safe in the care of our devoted servants. That is the first thing you need to know." He looked up and fixed his gaze on Geoffrey.

"The next thing is that my quest these weeks has been directed at finding them a cure, for I believe the sickness they suffer is the result of a centuries-old curse, and the challenge that I, Robert and Mary here have accepted, is to break that curse."

He then told the tale of the Broken Sword, from the battle of Boroughbridge, through to the theft by the brigand and so on to the journey that brought us to Harwich. Throughout the tale Geoffrey kept stealing glances at me, and when I slew the brigand, his jaw dropped. Then, when the story reached the part where I went down the well to retrieve the Broken Sword, his eyes seemed be coming clean out of their sockets.

"Is this true?" he whispered to me.

"It tells the story," I muttered.

"Not the half of it," said Robert. "Mary and Father carried my prostrate body some hundreds of yards and beat her step-father to the gate by the tiniest of margins."

"I can see why you then were married," said Geoffrey with a smile. "Although it must have been in quite a hurry. Were the banns not read?"

"Such matters can be managed," muttered Sir John with a sly nod that could have meant anything.

Geoffrey shrugged, then Sir John picked up his tale again,

finishing with the best piece of theatre – he reached into his bag and produced the very hilt that lay at the heart of his story.

As he held it aloft, sending shafts of gold, ruby and emerald light around the room, there was no doubt that he had achieved the same effect with Geoffrey as he had with me back in the Essex forest.

"By Heaven!" the merchant exclaimed. "'Tis a thing of wonder indeed. There is no doubt that restoring it to its rightful place will lift this dreadful curse."

"Aye," I answered, pleased that the topic of my supposed and highly irregular marriage was passed, "but we have now got Sir Reginald, his existing men, and most likely Tobias Whyte and his companions, standing between us and the restoration."

"True," said Geoffrey, drawing the word out as if it had many syllables. "There is only one way to solve this."

Robert, Sir John and I exchanged curious glances, as Geoffrey stood and walked to the fine wood-panelled door.

"Mildred!" he called. "Mildred, we need you here!"

As he returned to his chair, he observed, "In my many years of marriage, I can honestly say that there is no problem too great, no conundrum too complex, that my dear wife could not answer it in an instant." He sat, taking a sip of wine with the air of a man who had already solved the problem. I wondered what his wife Mildred could be like. I was imagining a tall, serious woman with a high brow and a commanding presence.

The person who entered a few moments later, was nothing of the sort.

She was small, slight and rosy-cheeked, smiling nervously after being summoned so brusquely, trying to wipe her hands on her apron and to tuck wisps of grey hair under her cotton coif at the same time.

"Yes, Geoffrey, my love?" she asked, glancing quickly at the rest of us.

"We have need of your council, my sweetness," he replied, as she found a seat.

Geoffrey introduced us all, then gave his version of Sir John's tale, ending with a nod to the other man to produce the Broken Sword, which he did with a flourish.

Mildred took it and turned it over in her lap, letting the fiery light of the gold and gems once more dance around the room. I could see the centuries-old magic of the piece begin to work on her, and before too long she put it down and looked at each of us with a satisfied smile.

"You need to avoid these many men who would stop you returning this piece to its rightful place?" she asked. I nodded. "And this place is in Nacton, on the far bank, a few leagues up the River Orwell?" Again I nodded, keen to know her plan. "And these men know where you are, even now?" She looked around the room with a small smile. She was aware, I am sure, that we were all desperate to hear what she had in mind, but it seemed she would first need to make sure she had all the facts straight.

Geoffrey nodded as well. "We believe so, if Mary's assertion is correct that Tobias Whyte and his drinking companions have joined this man Sir Reginald. Tobias knows me and where I live."

"We must assume so." She looked up from the Broken

Sword and said, "Geoffrey, be so good as to observe the lane opposite. The moon is full, so you will spot anyone watching the house."

Geoffrey opened a shutter by the smallest amount and put his eye to the window. "Aye," he said, "there is a man standing by the doorway opposite." He peered some more. "If I were to put a wager on it, I would say the odds are that it is young Whyte himself."

"Then we are sure," said Mildred. "But it is good. It plays well into my plan."

She leaned forward, her eyes reflecting the flickering flames from the grate.

"Then this is what we will do…"

16

CHAPTER SIXTEEN

It was in the soft orange glow of dawn three days later, that the tall, thick-set man who had been watching the house suddenly straightened up, quivering like a hunting dog scenting a deer, as three hooded figures slipped out onto the lane. He watched them scuttling from house to house in the shadows, until they were some twenty yards away. Without glancing back, he set off in pursuit.

I waited a few minutes until all four were fully out of sight, then I turned from the open window to Robert and Sir John who were standing behind me. "So it worked exactly as Mildred planned," I said.

"It was fortunate that in their build, Geoffrey, Mildred and their servant Daniel are a close match to each of us," said Sir John. "That watcher thought he was the clever one to spot them, but in truth, he was the fool."

Robert said nothing. He had the look of a man who was

chewing on a wasp, and he was avoiding my eye. I ignored him. Relations between us had once again become most sour, and I was not prepared to concede just now.

"And when they get to the docks," continued Sir John, seemingly oblivious to the frost between his son and me, although it must have been obvious from the strained silence when we broke fast earlier, "and when the watcher has called all his fellow pursuers to the scene, he will be red in the face." He chuckled to himself. "He will have brought them to ambush a local merchant, his wife and their servant going about their legitimate business, rather than stopping us trying to board a boat bound for the River Orwell."

"Come," I said, "they are gone. We should make our own way now." I picked up my bag and made for the door. "The boatman hired by Geoffrey will be waiting for us at the Dovercourt landing stage, and it will only be a matter of time until Sir Reginald realises they have been tricked, and starts sending men to seek us out."

I took a final look around the house that had been our home for the last three days; a welcome place of refuge from our dogged pursuers with some happy laughter, fine foods and restful sleep. How fortunate that Geoffrey had happened upon us in the Three Cups, and had been a friend of Sir John's. Although it was less fortunate that he had assumed I was Robert's bride – and even less fortunate that we had let him think so for such a time, that we could not now tell him the truth.

But the person most affected by this was Robert, for whom it seemed that the line between falsehood and reality was becoming blurred.

He had started behaving as if I had not only accepted his proposal, but we were already husband and wife. In the company of the Simmonds this was perfectly acceptable, for it maintained the conceit that we had married in haste a few days before. I could not fault his attentive and loving ways in public. He was always ensuring I was comfortable, such as if I tried to sit in whatever constricting gown Mildred had found for me, or even to breathe. He was forever fetching a glass of wine if I gave but the smallest of coughs or cleared my throat, in case I might be thirsty. He would complement me on my looks by daylight, by firelight, by moonlight, by candlelight… No, I could not fault his act as my husband in company.

My concern went deeper than that; my concern was that he had been slipping into the role in private – and worse still, that I was doing so as well.

I would have expected the mask to drop the moment we were away from the others, but our behaviour in our chamber, or when we strolled arm in arm in the small gardens, was no different. The concern for my welfare continued unchanged, and I found myself accepting, nay expecting, such attention.

In truth, I had little understanding of how a husband and wife should behave to each other. My stepfather had no wife, so there was nothing to observe there, and as Sir Reginald had promised only misery, I did not think him worthy as a guide. So when Robert treated me as a gentleman treats a lady, I could not help but be flattered into thinking that maybe he might be the man for me after all.

Of course, there was one element of our supposed

marriage that did not happen – and that was relations in the bedchamber.

I will admit that it did come very close, and if I had not been so mindful of the reality of our situation at the very last minute, things could have taken a very different turn.

Which, unfortunately, led directly to the present coldness in our relations.

It was the evening before, and we had finished a fine supper of roast venison with the Simmonds and Sir John. Mildred had been setting out once more the detail of her plans, and we had been making sure we knew all its parts.

I was sitting next to Robert as Mildred explained how we would make our way to Nacton without travelling through the docks at Harwich. Suddenly I felt Robert's hand seek mine under the table and hold it firmly. It was warm and strong, and I drew such comfort from his touch, that I found myself stroking the back of his hand with my thumb, just as he had done that evening in the Three Cups.

How far he had come since being Weed in the forest!

Indeed, he had now gained so much in confidence that he was truly becoming a real man. He was now seeming to appreciate and value his father greatly; agreeing with Sir John's statements and being most attentive to his needs. I could not deny that I was beginning to find this change of demeanour rather attractive.

It was after the meal had ended and the others were elsewhere, that Robert and I found ourselves seated alone by the fire. As we watched the flickering flames I leaned in close, and in the moment it seemed right to hold hands again.

Then I felt his head turn and I could feel his eyes observing me closely.

"There is some hair trying to escape from under your hood," he whispered, then he tried unsuccessfully to push it back again.

I giggled, making him giggle also.

"It cannot be held in," I said.

"Like its mistress."

"Indeed."

He was silent a moment, and I felt him turn back and look again into the fire.

There was a long pause, then he whispered again, "If it were only just your hair that escapes me."

I turned to look at him directly, put my finger on his lips and smiled. "Shush, my love. Let us not talk in such a way."

He rested his hand on my cheek and I let my head fall onto it, as we both stared again into the fire.

"My love?" he breathed quietly.

"A figure of speech," I answered, my gaze fixed on the flames.

"One I can wholeheartedly agree with," he responded, his other hand moving onto my knee.

I was silent, trying to think of something to say that would reflect the confusion I was in. For while my head was telling me that a free-spirited girl like me should be looking to a future that was fully in my own control, my heart was starting to have other ideas.

It seemed to be coming round to the notion that I could perhaps find happiness as the contented wife of Robert

Fitzwilliam, being cared for and protected as part of a loving family, and while there may not be such freedom for me as I was planning, maybe the care and protection would be acceptable as compensation.

Sir John came in. "I warrant you two are tired and should be abed," he said, observing us with a sly grin. "We have a big day ahead of us tomorrow, if Mistress Simmonds's plan is to succeed."

"My hand is asleep already," Robert chuckled, easing it gently from under my cheek, and we both stood. Then we bade Sir John good night and retired to our chamber.

As we entered, Robert immediately took my head in both his hands.

Our eyes locked as our lips started to move closer, drawn together by the pull of his hands – or was it by the movement of my head?

Our lips touched and it was as though a flame had suddenly come alight between us; a flame that could only be doused by our tongues as our mouths opened and they explored each other with a desperate urgency.

His hands slipped away from my head and started to move to my waist, pulling our bodies closer together. Then his lips came away from mine and moved down to my neck, lighting another flame there that now burned through my whole body.

I gasped as he slipped one hand under my bottom and lifted me with surprising strength, so he was carrying me in both his arms. He took me over to the bed, pushed me through the hangings and placed me down on my back, then stood over me with a look that was at once incredibly intense, yet at the same time, most tender.

In that moment I knew I wanted more than anything else in the world to learn the mysteries of love-making with him, right then, right there.

He had lit a flame within me and it burned hot.

What better way to discover these things than with a man who had found such a way to my heart? We would explore them together, for I felt sure this would be the first time for him as well.

I pulled him down onto me, feeling the weight of him pushing me into the bed, as our lips met again and our tongues sought each other out once more.

As he moved his hand under my gown and began to stroke my leg with long, slow movements that progressed ever closer to the top of my thigh, he let our lips part and I heard him say, almost as if to himself, "Yes. It is yes. Now we will truly be wed…"

Then it was as if someone had suddenly thrown open a curtain and blinding light burst in. The heat left me in an instant, and it was as if I was suddenly made of ice.

I rolled out from beneath him. I had not accepted his proposal. We were not betrothed, let alone married. If he did not recognise that, then I most certainly did.

"This is madness," I said. "We cannot do this."

"Why not?"

"Because we are not wed," I said, as if explaining to a small child why it could not have a sweet comfit.

His response was indeed childlike. "But I want to!" He

chewed on his lower lip as he regarded me. "And I thought you did too."

"Maybe I did," I answered. "But that does not change our situation." I paused. "I did not say yes. We are not wed, Robert. This is an act. It is not real."

"It was real enough just now. For both of us. I would we do it, now." He put a hand to my shoulder as if to hold me still. With a quick angry move I rolled away again. "No!" I repeated. "I said no!"

After a moment he gave a grunt, got up off the bed and started to peel off his clothes, with short, fierce movements.

I could see this conversation was going round in circles. "Listen to me," I snapped, as I stood and faced him. He paused, his hose around his knees. "We are not wed," I repeated. "One day, maybe we shall be, and then we can do… that." I pointed back at the bed.

He finished peeling off his hose and rolled the garment up carefully, but said nothing. "Did you hear me?" I asked. "I said that maybe…"

"I heard you," he interrupted. "And I take comfort that we may be wed at some future date, should the great Mary Fox deign to accept my proposal."

I could not think of a suitable reply, so in silence we prepared for bed, and slept facing away from each other.

---O---

And now we were making ready to leave the house, while there was a frost between us that would have iced up the Thames.

"Come," I said, looking at Sir John, "we must make haste."

He nodded and picked up his own bag. "Do not tarry, Robert," he said, casting a glance back at his son, who was standing by the door with the look of a man who was rooted to the spot like an oak sapling. "Make a move, boy."

With a sigh, Robert made for the front door after us. I waited as he passed through, ignoring me as if I did not exist. I closed it behind him, then locked it with the spare key given to me by Geoffrey, which I hid behind a loose brick as instructed.

I gestured to the men to wait as I looked up and down the lane, seeking out any unexpected shadows or shapes in doorways, but there was nothing to cause concern.

"Come," I said, and led them out, taking the opposite direction to the one that the Simmonds and their pursuer had taken earlier. We hurried to the end of the lane, before turning onto the road that would take us out of Harwich and on to the coastal path, ending up at the same little Dovercourt dock where we had made landfall a few days earlier.

As we walked, I continually glanced behind us, looking for the movement of any pursuer; at one point stopping as I thought I saw something, but it was only the dawn sun flashing as someone opened a diamond-paned window.

"There is no pursuer," snapped Robert, as I caught him up again.

"I need to be certain."

"There are bound to be people about, even this early in the morning."

"Yet we have not seen another soul since we left the house," I pointed out.

As if on cue, a pair of small boys emerged from a passage between two houses. They gave us a strange look, then hurried past. I looked back at them, meeting the gaze of one over his shoulder.

I shuddered. Why were they showing such an interest in us?

"What is it?" asked Sir John, the concern on his face no doubt mirroring my own.

"Those boys," I said. "There was something about them."

"'Tis nothing," muttered Robert.

"Nay," answered his father. "If Mary is concerned, then so am I."

"Aye." Robert stopped in the road. "If the great Mary Fox is concerned, then we should all be."

"Robert!" Sir John snapped. "Do not talk to Mary like that." He paused, looking from Robert to me with a frown. "What is the matter with you two this morning?"

"There is naught," I assured him. "Let us be off."

"Lovers' tiff, eh?" asked Sir John. "Well, you had better make up shortly, for I will not be in the middle of that." He strode off ahead of us, as if to make his point even clearer.

We followed and walked in an uncomfortable silence for a further half hour, until we had covered most of the coastal path and the Dovercourt landing stage was nearly in sight.

It seemed to me that this silence should end; we should not make the next step of this journey with this animosity hanging over us like a grey cloud.

I put my hand on Robert's arm. "Now listen..." I began.

He stopped abruptly. "No, you listen, Mary Fox!" he interrupted. "You listen to me!"

It appeared that an emotional dam had been breached, as if while we walked he had been rehearsing over and over what he would say, and needed but the smallest excuse for it to flood out.

"This past week I have taken instructions from a woman," he said, his face turning a deep shade of red, "and a mere slip of a girl at that. I have gone along with it because I believed, rightly or wrongly, that you knew what you were doing."

I stayed silent, looking to see where this was going.

"Yet somehow, some way, I found myself falling under your spell, and as we were pretending to be married, I came to tell myself that we really were so." He shook his head. "More fool me." He stared down at me as we walked. "So when I had it made plain to me, plainer than the nose on my face, that we are not wed, and may never be, then I had to…" he stopped in the road as he appeared to seek the right word, "…I had to adjust my expectations." He marched on again, so I had to trot after him, nearly tripping over in my Mildred Simmonds gown. "So I will thank you, Mistress Mary Fox, if I do not immediately come round to your way of thinking. Rather, I need time to change my thinking to match yours." He snorted like a bad-tempered pony and added over his shoulder. "If ever I do."

"Wait!" I snapped, stopping in the road and standing with my hands upon my hips. "You wait there, Master Robert Fitzwilliam!"

He also stopped and slowly turned.

I knew that my blood was also up and if I did not guard my tongue I would most likely say what I truly felt – that he was acting as a spoiled child and going the best way to lose my affections completely. But such things would not help relations between us. Nor would it help lead to the return of the Broken Sword, and the restoration to health of the innocent women of his family. So I decided on a different course and took a deep breath.

"Robert, whatever you may think of me, I am truly proud of you."

"Eh?" He was clearly not expecting that.

I pressed on, briefly noting that up ahead, Sir John had also stopped and was now watching us with a raised eyebrow. "Yes, I am proud of how you have become braver, more resourceful, more understanding and altogether a better person than the weed..." I took another breath, "than the cowardly fellow I first encountered in the forest..."

His eyes narrowed as he considered my words, and his colour started to return to its normal pale pink.

"...so I ask only that you leave that fellow behind in the forest where he belongs, and show me that the new, stronger and braver Robert Fitzwilliam is here to stay."

"I do not seek your pride," he muttered, but I could see he said it with less conviction than before. Perhaps I was getting through.

"But you have it nonetheless." I pressed my advantage. "I may be just a slip of a girl, but I have had my share of challenges. So I know bravery when I see it, and I have seen more of it in you these last few days."

He was about to answer, and I could see the thoughts working across his face as he considered his options, but then something over my shoulder caught his eye.

All the colour drained from his face in an instant, like a tankard of ale being emptied.

He pointed behind me and said, "horse… horsemen! There are horsemen coming!" He then turned and started to run up the path, nearly knocking down his father as he went past.

I glanced back, and indeed, there were horsemen riding hard along the path maybe half a mile behind us, kicking up a cloud of dust.

Sir John called to me, "Come, Mary, quick!"

I pulled my skirts up and ran as hard as I could for the landing stage.

Suddenly it did not seem so close; it was almost as if it was receding as we ran, and in desperation I glanced back. Now I could clearly see that there were four of them, crouched low over the necks of their horses.

Damn those two boys in Harwich! It must have been them who reported on us! They must have been sent to check in case we employed the very same trickery that Mildred had planned, and now Sir Reginald and his men were almost upon us!

And we had spent so much time stopping and arguing that they were able to catch us…

I turned back, put my head down and ran as fast as I could. Now I could hear the hooves pounding and the cries of our pursuers close behind us, so that fear lent me wings on my feet and I ran like Hermes himself.

"Come, Mary!" called Sir John again. I looked up. Heaven be praised, he was actually on the landing stage! Robert was already clambering into a small boat with a single triangular lateen sail.

I ran onto the landing stage myself and Sir John grabbed my arm and fairly threw me into the boat, then jumped in himself, shouting, "Cast away, fellow! Cast away!"

The boatman pulled his tethering rope into the boat, then turned its bow away from the landing stage, just as Sir Reginald clattered to a stop above us, his horse blowing hard.

The boat leant over as the sail caught the wind and it started to move quickly away from the land, just as the slight figure of Tobias Whyte appeared beside Sir Reginald, steam rising from his horse's flanks.

Now we were some twenty or so yards from the landing stage, and the other two riders pulled up. All four stayed on their horses, observing us without words as the boatman put further distance between ourselves and them.

"That was close, indeed," said Sir John, voicing the thought in all our minds.

The boatman, a weathered old fellow in a grey cap with a fine white beard, said, "Those men would have done you harm?"

"Yes," I answered. "They would have dragged me away with them."

"And perhaps done my father and me to death," added Robert.

We all looked back at the landing stage. They were still there, like four stone statues.

"Then you are well away from them," the boatman said. "But it is fortunate they do not urge their beasts into the water, for it is still shallow enough for them to ride out to where we are now."

I thought Robert was going to heave up as he stared at the man.

The boatman chuckled. "Fear not, young fellow. We will be well out to the deep water soon, so there is scant chance they will catch us that way."

Robert did not look particularly reassured. "Are you certain?"

"Aye, fear not. We will be in Walton ere long, and you can rest easy."

I looked back. The four were turning their horses and urging them to a canter back towards Harwich.

"Mary?" said Sir John with a half-smile.

"Yes?"

"What exactly were you saying earlier? Something about Robert being brave?"

17

CHAPTER
SEVENTEEN

The plan that Mildred Simmonds had set out was, in essence, very simple and in the main it had worked well. If, that is, you ignored the mad scrabble for the landing stage just ahead of Sir Reginald and his men.

Mildred, Geoffrey and Daniel their servant had succeeded in fooling the watcher – who I think was one of Tobias Whyte's drinking companions – into believing they were us three. So drawing him away from the house had been easy, and allowed us to slip off in the other direction.

The timing of the plan was critical. It was important that the decoys arrived at Harwich docks shortly before the departure of the *Kynborow*, a small coastal vessel bound for Ipswich. As she was the only boat making this trip up the

Orwell for several days, her sailing would naturally cause Sir Reginald and his men to be on the lookout.

Then, when they were at the docks, the Simmonds trio were planning to throw off their hoods and walk openly into a tavern for a hearty breakfast, thus showing the watchers that they had wasted all this time pursuing the wrong quarry.

Meanwhile, we were making contact with the white-bearded boatman hired to sail us across the estuary to the harbour at Walton, whence we would secure horses from a friend of Geoffrey, and ride at speed to Nacton.

It was unfortunate that we had been seen by those two boys, who must have been instructed to hide in an alleyway further up the lane and report back if anyone matching our descriptions passed them by.

No, now I thought on it, it was more than unfortunate, it was a serious blow to our plans. For now Sir Reginald had seen us sailing out into the estuary. He would have had no trouble deducing that we were bound for Walton as the boat was too small to sail up the river, and so were planning to journey on to Nacton over land. If he had access to a boat, or was prepared to ride hard for the bridge at Ipswich, he could still cut us off.

Such thoughts troubled me greatly as we headed into the open waters of the estuary and the wind started to strengthen, causing the boat to lean hard over and to rise and fall across ever larger waves.

The boatman seemed unaffected by the increasing violence of the seas, and gave me a broad grin as he pushed on the tiller.

"Gets a bit fresher out here," he shouted. "Though I warrant your companion is not enjoying it greatly!" He gestured at Sir John, who was leaning over the side, spewing occasionally into the sea.

Robert was not so afflicted. "What say you?" he shouted at me, as the boat crashed its bows into the valley between two waves, then climbed back up to the summit of the next one.

"About what, exactly?" I yelled back.

"Our current situation."

I chose to misunderstand. "The wind is fierce," I said, "but we are well placed to arrive within a reasonable time."

"I know that," he snapped. "I meant, what of our departure under the watchful eye of your would-be husband?" He observed me with as much dispassion as was possible while we were both being tossed about like two acorns in a drum. "How do you plan to get us out of danger this time?"

"I know not," I responded. "But I am sure I will think of something."

"Please do."

I let this ride a while; partly because I wanted to consider how best to resolve the frost between us, but mainly because it was now too windy to hold any sort of meaningful conversation.

Eventually we arrived in calmer waters outside the entrance to the harbour. It was a welcome relief as the wind dropped, the waves softened, and the boat was once again nearly upright. We slid slowly towards the village, with its cluster of buildings around a welcoming little pier.

The boatman started to busy himself with ropes, while Sir John stared glassy-eyed at the shore.

I chose this moment to continue the interrupted conversation with Robert.

"I value your friendship more than your enmity," I said. "What would you have me do?"

He was silent a while, and I began to think that perhaps he had not heard.

"I have made you an offer of marriage," he said eventually. "And I would you think on it with the greatest of care, then give me your firm answer, so I know where we stand."

I nodded, glad he had made his feeling so clear. I resolved therefore to help him as best I could. "That I will, as soon as I have decided," I said. "Please be assured it is uppermost in my mind, and I will let you know my decision soon."

"Good." He gave a small smile, which I took to be a sign that maybe the frost was thawing a little more.

"So let us be friends," I said, then decided to press a little further. "We have no need for any deception, now we are away from Geoffrey and Mildred." I said. "So perhaps it can be as before?"

"Aye, perhaps." He gave me a long, searching stare as we sailed towards the pier. His gaze held me with such intensity, that I was wholly unprepared for the bump of the boat coming to a stop, and even though it was not a particularly hard landing, it threw me forward into his arms. For a brief moment he held me tight, then he kissed me gently on the forehead, before putting me down. "Aye," he repeated. "We shall be friends, so that your decision is made on the best of evidence."

So the frost was over – for that I was most glad. But when

I thought of saying 'yes' to his proposal, once again there was a feeling like lead in my belly…

Sir John coughed and stood up, clutching at the rough column of the pier for support

"Landfall," he muttered. "I ne'er thought I would once again see land." He turned to Robert. "If I ever, ever express a willingness to go to sea again, be sure to stop me." He clambered up some steps attached to the pier and struggled onto the wooden platform. Robert followed, and after I had settled the fare with the boatman, I climbed the steps as well.

We watched the boat bear away again, leaning over as its sail caught a new breeze; the boatman standing proud in the stern like a solid grey statue silhouetted against the bright shimmering water.

I suggested we wait a few minutes for Sir John to recover his balance and his stomach – a suggestion with which he found great favour, so I settled myself on a stone bench and dug into my bag for a packet containing some bread and cheese, as well as a costrel of wine.

Robert sat next to me, and produced a similar packet and costrel from his bag.

"Some bread, father?" he offered.

"Nay," said Sir John, eying up the bread with a jaundiced look. "My constitution is not yet ready for that." He paused and swallowed heavily and a look of panic appeared on his white face. "Oh, by the Heavens!" He suddenly ran to the edge of the dock and leaned over. Robert and I glanced uneasily at each other, as the sound of dry retching could be heard.

I nodded to Robert. "I warrant he could use your assistance."

"Aye," he said, and went over to help his father.

I took a bite of my cheese, and was quietly observing Robert holding Sir John by the waist as he leaned again over the water, when I became aware of a man approaching the bench and sitting down next to me.

I finished my cheese, slipped the packet back into my bag, then glanced briefly across. He was an older fellow, I guessed of a similar age to Sir John, but more broadly built. His hair and beard were grey and not well trimmed, and his woollen cap was faded and misshapen.

"Your companion will never make a sailor," the man observed, staring at Sir John. His voice was low and reminded me of walking across a beach of coarse pebbles. "That is the worst case of sea-sickness I have seen this many a year."

He turned to me and I gasped despite myself. His left eye was bright blue, while his right was milky white, dissected by a thick red scar that ran from his hairline, down his cheek and into his beard.

"Jacob Cruddon, at your service, mistress," he said.

I forced my gaze away from the damaged eye. "Mary Fox," I replied. He nodded and turned away again. Further comment seemed to be called for, so I ventured, "And what might that service be, Master Cruddon?"

There was a pause as he seemed to gather his thoughts. "You and your companions all carry bags, and have come ashore from a boat that immediately returns to sea?"

"Indeed," I answered, unsure where this was going.

"So I take it you are travellers on the road, making your way someplace?" He turned the eye on me again. "Shall I hazard Ipswich?" I must have given him a blank look. "Or perhaps you venture north, to Woodbridge?"

"Neither," I said, "but you are right that we are travellers."

"And the man who is such a poor sailor," he asked, pointing at Sir John. "Your father?"

I shook my head. "You ask too many questions, sir." I forced myself to look only at the working eye. "I would know what is your purpose?"

He laughed, making the good side of his face crinkle, while the scarred side did not move. It gave him the look of a man with two faces.

"I beg your pardon. You must think me most forward, young mistress!" He paused again. "I am in the business of making your journey better. If you would go on foot, I can make it swifter, and if you would already go on horseback, I can make it safer."

"Safer?"

He laughed again. "Your question tells me much. By ignoring my offer of speed and leaping directly to my offer of safety, you make it clear that you were already preparing to travel on horseback." I said nothing, so he continued, "I know these parts well, and can say for sure that all roads that run through the woodlands from here are crawling with cut-purses, brigands and thieves, just as the back of the dog crawls with fleas. Whichever way you and your companions are bound, you will inevitably come across such bands of men. You will be robbed at the very least, and at worst," he paused, his good eye fixed on mine, "you will be killed."

I forced myself to maintain calm. "I am aware of such brigands, sir, and my companions and I are well able to defend ourselves. Indeed," I could not help but add, "we have already met with one such fellow, and I can assure you, we came off the best."

"I am sure you did, young mistress," he answered, "for I can see there is fire in your eye, and perhaps you are even well practiced with a sword…" I shivered as the image of the original brigand's dying face suddenly appeared again in front of me. "…but," Cruddon continued, "these men are equally well practiced. Their skills are in concealment, ambush and surprise. You will not know they are even there, before they have thrown you from your horses, taken everything down to your last button, and left you for dead."

He made a point, as I had heard of such bands of villains, living outside of the laws and customs of society, robbing travellers and even killing them if they put up any form of resistance. It would indeed be the cruellest of fortune if we were to get this close to returning the Broken Sword, only to have it stolen once again. Or worse.

"So what would you do to protect us?" I asked.

He raised an eyebrow. "I would first ask your menfolk, naturally."

I let this pass. "Then what?"

"I would put you in a sturdy carriage pulled by a pair of strong horses, and I would ride ahead myself, so I could defend you if – or indeed, when – attackers appear. But not only that," he leaned forward, "I would also bring another man to ride beside the carriage. So there would be three of us, including the carriage driver. That way you and your companions would be fully protected and able to reach your destination unharmed."

"That sounds most reassuring," I said, as Robert led Sir John back to the bench. "I am sure there is a charge for this service?"

"What service is that?" asked Sir John. He was thankfully looking more his normal colour.

Once I had introduced Master Cruddon and he had again explained his offer to the men, Sir John repeated my question. "Pray tell, sir, what is the charge?"

"Twenty shillings," came the reply.

I looked at Sir John and could see he was thinking the same as me – that this was a reassuring amount. Any less and it would seem like Cruddon did not care for the money, which would suggest he was planning to steal from us himself. Any more, and it would seem like he was simply being greedy, and not expecting us to hire him.

"And if we do agree to this?" Sir John asked. "What happens then?"

Cruddon gave his lopsided smile. "Then I will bring the carriage here in an hour, and we shall begin our journey."

I kept silent a while, trying to decide if we were more at risk or less if we took up this man's offer.

"What say you?" demanded Cruddon to Sir John.

"Wait," I answered. "We must discuss." I gestured to Robert and Sir John to walk a few yards away with me. "I trust the man no further than I could throw him," I said, once we were out of his hearing. "But I have heard tell of such cut-purses and brigands, so maybe his protection is warranted."

"If we are attacked and he defends us, then we are better off," observed Sir John. "If we are attacked and he does not defend us, then we are no worse off." He paused. "Apart from twenty shillings, of course."

"So you say we should accept?" asked Robert.

"I say we should, but I also say we keep our hands on our swords and do not let our guard drop for a moment," answered his father.

"I agree," I said. "We were lucky with the first brigand; we should not assume such luck again."

We returned to Cruddon. "I accept your offer," I said. "We will be here in an hour, and we are headed to Nacton."

Cruddon looked at Sir John, his good eyebrow raised. "You agree this also?" he asked. "With this woman who speaks as your leader?"

"Aye, I do. What of it?"

"Nothing." Cruddon shrugged. "I have ne'er seen a woman with such authority over men, 'tis all."

Robert gave a sharp breath. "Mary is as good as any man with a sword. She dispatched a brigand a few days since. Ran him right through. We tossed his body into the trees. Do not think she is just a mere woman."

The older man looked Robert up and down, almost as if he had only just noticed him. "Indeed, young fellow. I mark it well." He shifted his gaze to me, becoming more to the point. "Right. I will see you here in an hour, when I have gathered my men." I nodded. "Farewell, Mary the leader. We will be on our travels immediately on my return, so do not let your menfolk wander off." With a chuckle at his own joke, he crossed to where a horse was tethered, mounted and rode away.

An hour later we were back on the same spot, having

passed the time in a nearby tavern, still convincing ourselves over some ale that we were making the right decision. I had also changed out of the constricting gown I had been wearing, and resumed my more normal attire of breeches and a plain jerkin top.

Cruddon rode up with a carriage behind him, drawn as he had said, by two strong horses. A rough-looking man was sitting in the front holding the reins, while another such man followed on horseback. The carriage looked very basic; a simple open box with a bench front and back, with a small door on each side and a pair of wheels secured under the front and rear. Certainly, it was nothing like the fine carriage my stepfather used to travel into London, with its silk upholstered seats and leather straps by the wheels to soften the bumps in the road.

The men looked as hard and as rough as Cruddon himself, and again I asked myself if we were doing the right thing.

"Get in," Cruddon said, after dismounting and holding open the small door to the carriage.

As I climbed in he observed, "I see you dress now more like the man you act."

I ignored this, and we settled ourselves on the bench seats; me and Robert taking the rear bench, while Sir John sat facing us with his back to the horse.

Cruddon came up and leaned on the side of the carriage beside me. "I will have ten shillings now." He held out a calloused hand. "The rest when we arrive at your journey's end."

I undid my belt and slid off the tan leather purse branded with the Saxon device. His eye widened slightly when he saw it, but he said nothing as I counted out the coins and handed them over. He selected one and bit it, his eye never leaving mine. It must have passed his test, as he then poured all the coins into his own black leather purse and mounted his horse.

"Away!" he called, and with a creak of the carriage wheels and a crack of the reins from the driver, we set off.

18

CHAPTER EIGHTEEN

The first part of the journey was along a single track cutting through open fields, with the afternoon sun giving us warmth and farmland birds providing a pleasing musical accompaniment. I noted the shrill cry of the lapwing, the fine melody of the linnet and the trill of the bunting, as well as the occasional song of the thrush and sparrow.

Such sounds brought me back to Marchington Manor, and the times when I would be in my chamber, undisturbed by my brothers or my stepfather. I would sit by the open window on a summer's evening and listen to the birdsong outside. It was always a welcome moment of peace and tranquillity, and would occasionally be made even more special by a visit from Rufus, the friendly robin with a bright red breast, coming to my window for scraps of bread. He was a confident little fellow with an inquisitive eye, who would land on my sill and observe me with interest, and even once or twice, stand on my hand and peck bread from my open palm.

I wondered where Rufus was now? Perhaps he had found another girl at another window, and I was but a distant memory.

I smiled to myself. Or maybe he had followed me all the way from Essex like a guardian angel, and was even now flying overhead, scouting the path in front of us for dangerous cut-purses and preparing to fly in their faces to distract them from their evil intent.

I sighed. No, it would not be a guardian angel who would come to my aid if needed.

I looked at the broad back of Jacob Cruddon ahead of the carriage, ambling along on his horse as if without a care, my ten shillings clinking in his purse, and the expectation of ten more later. Would it be him? Would he truly protect us, or was he preparing to double-cross us in some way?

Robert and Sir John were each looking out of the carriage, no doubt lost in their own thoughts as we bumped along.

I glanced at the other ruffian riding closely alongside us. He was cut from the same cloth as Cruddon; a man with the experience of age rather than the fire of youth, but still with the ability and intent to fight, by the look of him.

He gave me a broken-toothed smile – one that made him seem even more evil. I quickly looked away, and chose instead to study my hands in my lap. I waited a few moments then looked back. He was still giving me his smile, but now with an added leer that made me feel sick.

I looked quickly away again, concerned in case he thought I was flirting with him. I glanced down at my feet on the rough floorboards, and drew a sudden breath. There was something most interesting; the path could clearly be seen passing below us as we jolted along. There were wide gaps between the boards, where the wood had rotted and fallen away, such that it was a wonder that the floor had held our weight as we had got in earlier. I pushed my foot on the nearest board and felt it crack slightly.

"Art well, Mary?" asked Sir John.

"Aye," I answered, and was about to point out my discovery, when I realised that the fellow beside us could hear every word – and was listening intently. I held Sir John's gaze a moment, then made an eye across at the man, to ensure Sir John knew I had a concern we could be overheard. "I am enjoying the ride and looking forward to arriving," I said clearly.

He followed my eye and nodded slightly. "Indeed," he exclaimed, with a sly glance back at the man himself. "This is an altogether better way to travel."

Robert turned to us, then shook his head. "I would we were through yonder forest already," he growled, pointing up the path where tall trees were gathered at the start of the woods and the light seemed to disappear as if into a black tunnel. "For I fear danger lurks… ow!" He broke off as I brought my heel down sharply on his shin. Sir John leaned across from opposite and patted him on the knee. "There, son, there is naught to fear, for we have protection." He slid his eye across to the rider beside us again, in an almost comical fashion. There was a moment where Robert looked blank, then it was as if a flame that had gone out suddenly sprang back to life.

"Ahh." He nodded. "Indeed," he said a little too loudly, "we shall be there in no time."

After that there seemed little point in conversation, so we remain silent, each lost in our own thoughts, and in my case, plans.

Soon we passed into the forest, and the warmth of the sun disappeared in an instant. As we continued on the path deeper and deeper into the forest, I shivered, and not just with the cold. The dark, oppressive trees loomed overhead, cutting out all the sunshine except the occasional flash from above. Instinctively my hand went to the hilt of my sword, and I shifted my position so I could draw it more easily.

I glanced at Sir John and saw he had done the same.

As we bumped along the path, I kept a constant watch to each side, noting how the shadows changed as we moved past, continually assessing that their shape matched the trees that made them; that it was not the shadow of a concealed attacker.

I looked up as well. Every overhanging branch could allow a cut-purse to lie in wait and drop down on us, so every time I saw such a branch in the distance, I paid it particular attention, searching the top for the shape of a prone man, or any unnatural movement.

I also listened hard to the sounds of the forest. There were many different bird calls, constantly echoing around us. Were they all real? Or was one a leader alerting his men that we were coming?

The ruffian that was paid to protect us was also casting his eyes left to right, and I could see from the movements of the driver's head, that he was doing the same.

The forest grew yet darker as we progressed deeper and deeper in, jolting along the path, all on the highest alert.

The shadows became blacker, making it harder to define what was a tree and what was the space between. I had just screwed my eyes, searching the darkness to my right for anything that was not as it should be, when I became aware of a something at the edge of my view. It seemed like a shape was moving alongside us, keeping pace.

I watched for a few moments, to see if it was just another shadow. But it was not. There was no doubt something – or someone – was tracking us.

"Beware yonder," I said.

"Where?" Sir John returned.

I inclined my head in the direction of the shape.

"I see it," he said. We watched for a few more moments, then we heard an unmistakable sound.

It was the noise of a twig snapping underfoot.

The ruffian beside us and the driver heard it too, as both looked quickly in the direction of the noise.

I stood, taking care to place my feet on a firm part of the floorboards, and drew my sword.

The shape could still be seen as a darker shadow keeping pace – but now it was closer.

It looked like a man crouching as he ran.

I gripped my hilt firmly, a bead of sweat on my brow and more starting to run down my back, as the shape moved closer, with more breaking branch sounds as it started to move ahead of us. Sir John also stood and drew his sword, and I saw the ruffian had his out as well, as the shape grew closer still...

And squealed. Then grunted.

A break in the trees let in a patch of sunlight, revealing the large black boar that had been running alongside us.

I sat heavily down on my seat, my sword still drawn.

"Garn!" yelled the driver, halting the horses. The ruffian dropped back behind the carriage, then came up along the other side and faced the boar with his sword low.

The boar stopped and lowered its head, so its evil-looking tusks were pointing squarely at the ruffian's horse.

Now I could make it out clearly, I could see just how big it was; standing as tall as the horse's chest. It pawed at the ground, giving a series of grunts, squeals and barks. If they were intended to scare its prey into submission, they certainly worked on me. The ruffian, however, stood his ground.

Then the boar charged.

As it thundered towards the ruffian he pulled his horse to one side, so the momentum of the boar carried it past him, close enough for him to make a short stabbing motion with his sword into the creature's back.

The boar squealed, then crashed off into the undergrowth, disappearing into the shadows behind us.

I breathed a huge sigh of relief, as the ruffian wheeled his horse round and trotted up alongside.

"Plenty of wild boar in these parts," he said. "Need to show them who has the sharpest point. Though their skin is thicker than ten hides of leather. Can only jab at them and it barely gives them a scratch.." He sheathed his sword. "Seen a boar kill a man before," he added. "Nasty mess."

I nodded, unable to speak.

"Was that a boar?" This was Cruddon, who had turned back and was now on our other side.

"Aye," said the ruffian. "Gave 'im a scratch with my point. Doubt he even felt it, his hide's that thick. But he might decide to 'ave another go."

"Indeed," said Cruddon. He turned to me. "So we should keep moving. And we need to be out of the forest before dusk."

The driver cracked his reins and the carriage lurched forward, as Cruddon trotted on and resumed his forward position.

"We are as nervous as kittens," observed Sir John with a smile, as once more we bumped and jolted through the dark forest.

"At least it was only a boar," said Robert. "And the fellow chased it off."

"Only a boar?" I exclaimed. "Did you not see the size of it?"

After that we proceeded in silence, with the ruffian beside me resuming his watch. For the first time since we climbed into the carriage, I let myself relax a little. The man had faced off the boar, which had demonstrated that he was prepared to protect us, so perhaps he and Cruddon were genuine.

I looked at Robert, his face flickering as the light changed.

I must not forget that he was waiting on my answer to his proposal.

A patch of clear sky illuminated his face in full, and he was smiling at me.

Could I accept? Could I become Mistress Fitzwilliam, dutiful wife and mother? Could I trade this new life I had found, this life of adventure and freedom, for convention and security? It would give me the protection afforded by Sir John and the Broken Sword. It would give me a mother in Lady Fitzwilliam, who I was sure would be lovely. I would get a sister, too.

Maybe that would be a fair exchange; my freedom in return for the family I never had before? To love and be loved in return – surely that was worth becoming the woman that met God's and society's expectations?

And yet – how could I ignore the feeling of lead in my belly whenever I thought of settling down? Surely this was God telling me something? Telling me that I was not born to be a wife and mother; rather that I was born to be a free spirit, unchecked by the conventions of society, able to go where I pleased and help where I could?

How would I feel if I said yes to Robert, and ignored God's plan for me?

With a sigh, I resolved to give this more thought once we had returned the Broken Sword and restored the family to health and fortune.

But first we had to get safely out of the forest.

Which meant we should be moving…

"Why have we stopped?" I demanded.

The ruffian said nothing. "I asked, why we have stopped, here in this clearing?"

Just then Cruddon rode up and brought his mount to a halt next to us. I repeated my question.

"Because I say so," Cruddon snarled.

My blood turned to ice as I stared at him.

This had always been his plan. After his empty promises; after that business with the boar that had given me false security, he had planned to double-cross us. Like as not there were no cut-purses or brigands – it was our protectors who planned to turn on us all along.

"You would rob us?" I whispered. His eye flicked briefly to the driver, who had turned in his seat and had his sword out. Then it flicked over to the ruffian, who had his blade out also. He nodded to each with what must have been the prearranged signal and said "Now!"

Which meant it was the time to put my own plan into action.

Fully drawing my sword as I stood, I screamed at Sir John, "Duck!"

Thankfully he did not question this, but bowed his head low.

I brought my blade round in a smooth, wide arc just above him, making contact with the driver's arm hard enough to go through and break the bone. The man screamed and dropped his sword.

As Cruddon and the ruffian stared at the driver, I stamped hard on the rotten boards of the carriage. They gave way immediately, sending me crashing to the ground underneath. I rolled quickly away from under the carriage, then thrust my sword tip up into the ruffian's foot. He let out a bellow that made his horse rear up in fright, sending him crashing down onto his back. I grabbed the sword that he dropped and flung it away across the forest, then brought my own blade down on his ankle. If I had been standing, and had my full height behind the blow, it would have severed his foot. As it was, it opened his leg right up, leaving him screaming and writhing on the ground.

As all this happened, Cruddon was still on his horse, so as I was dealing with his companion, he leapt down and raised his sword to impale me on the ground. I saw it coming and was able to roll aside just in time, so that it went into the earth with a sickening thud, exactly where my head had been.

As Cruddon pulled his blade out, I leapt to my feet and turned to face him.

"You can swing a sword, girl," he growled, "but can you fight?"

I backed away as he came after me, but my move was only to give myself open space.

As I stepped back Cruddon advanced on me with a furious look in his eye.

"You may be a slip of a girl, but I will kill you just like any man who crosses me," he said.

"I crossed you?" I answered, as I came into the guard position. "Nay, I believe it is the other way around. Your men would have robbed us. They had to be stopped."

"Ha!" he shouted. "You think this about them? Not at all!"

"Then what?" I answered, eyeing the ground in front of me for any roots or stones that could trip me up when the fight started. I noted that there was one on my left; a raised root running six or eight inches above the path from a stout oak trunk.

"This," Cruddon snarled, "is about my son."

I looked up. "Your what?"

"My son," he repeated. "My son who had a purse with a Saxon design that I had given him, and who disappeared a week or two ago near Maldon." He swept his sword through the air a few times. "My son who, I learned today, was killed and his poor body thrown into the undergrowth." He advanced a couple of steps. "By you, Mary Fox."

"He had robbed and was about to kill Sir John," I said.

"I care not for that. He lived outside the law." Again, he advanced. "But I do care when I find the person who is responsible, because that person still has his purse and their companion boasts how she has killed my son. So my plans today changed from robbery to revenge." He raised his sword. "That person has to die. You, Mary Fox, you have to die."

Then suddenly he advanced, and I found myself in a desperate fight for my life.

His blade was coming at me almost faster than the eye could see. I had to parry and turn it; my own blade taking blow after blow as he drove me back, but I managed to avoid ever giving him a chance to strike at my chest or head, keeping my responses as fast as his.

For a man with limited eyesight, he had an excellent ability to cut, sweep and thrust, but as he fought I began to see that he did have a weakness. It was a small thing at first, but as he came at me every time I could definitely see it. He could not place his feet – his stance was very poor. It was no doubt a consequence of his single vision – in that he could not easily see the ground at the same time as fight.

I resolved to use this weakness against him.

As he drove forward I suddenly gave ground. He lost his balance, tripping slightly, before recovering it again. I used this to my advantage, now pressing forward myself and starting to attack instead of defending, so that I soon had him falling back under my own onslaught. He was able to stop me getting a clear strike at his head or chest, and although I did create many chances, he always turned my blade at the last possible moment.

But now I had him close to the raised root.

Seizing the opportunity, I concentrated my attacks on his right side, so that he had to turn to defend it better, then I thrust for his chest, driving him back in the direction I wanted him to go. He turned my blade once again, and our swords locked.

His ugly face was so close that we were almost touching. "I did not mean to kill him," I gasped. "It was accidental."

"You lie," he snarled. "You have skill with the sword, as did he. So you would have fought him."

I could see that there was no point in continuing this, but I wanted to end it on my own terms.

So I stepped away.

With a look of triumph as he saw the opening, he swung his sword at my head. I dropped to one knee, the blade slicing through the air clean above me. This left his chest exposed, so jabbed up at him with my point. It was not a mortal blow, but it was enough to make him stagger back. His heel caught the root just as I had hoped. With a yell he overbalanced and fell, hitting his head a mighty crack on the tree behind.

As I watched, his eye rolled up, then he slid down the tree and was still.

There was a moment's peace, then Robert and Sir John appeared at my side.

"Well done, Mary!" said Sir John, as I stood panting with the exertion. "We would have joined the fray, but Robert here is quite incapable with a sword, and as you were holding him off so well, I was concerned it would have caused you a fatal distraction."

"But now he is at our mercy," said Robert, "we should finish him, and his wounded men as well. So let us now run them all through and be gone."

"No," I answered, sheathing my sword and looking from the ruffian on the ground clutching his ankle, to the driver lying in the carriage holding his arm, then back to Cruddon, unconscious at the base of the tree. "Let him be. Let them all be."

"Why? They would have robbed us, and no doubt killed us after. We should do them the same service."

"No," I repeated. "I would not kill them. We leave them here to take their chances, but we do not kill them in cold blood."

"I say we do." Robert drew his sword and advanced towards Cruddon. "Stand aside Mary. I will do this turncoat first, then I will see to the other two."

"I said no!" I stood in front of the prone body of Jacob Cruddon. "If you want to kill him, you will need to kill me first."

"Are you mad?" Robert snapped. "Not a minute ago you and he were fighting to the death – and now, when you have him at your mercy, you spare him?"

"I was fighting to save my own life, Robert, not to take his." I paused. "That brigand I killed on the day we met – that was his son. I will not be the cause of any further deaths in his family."

"Now you listen to me, girl…" Robert began, but Sir John raised his hand.

"Nay, Robert, if Mary says we leave them, then we leave them. Cruddon has been rendered unconscious and the other two have taken serious cuts. Their chances are slim as it stands, but Mary is right – we do not kill in cold blood. We are better than that."

"We will take the horses," I said, "and leave these men here. Maybe there are others who would have attacked us, although now I doubt it. But if there are, then they will find these three and no doubt come to their aid."

Robert scowled at us both, then marched over to the carriage without another word.

In uncomfortable silence Sir John, Robert and I mounted three of the horses. We moved slowly out of the clearing, leaving both the ruffian and the driver nursing their crudely bandaged wounds in the carriage, while Cruddon was still slumped against the tree.

I checked the Saxon purse at my belt. It was now joined by the black leather one of Cruddon's that contained my original ten shillings, as well as many more of his ill-gotten gains.

I squeezed my heels into the side of Cruddon's horse and urged it to trot towards Nacton.

19

CHAPTER NINETEEN

It was largely a silent journey out of the forest, with each of us lost in our own thoughts; the fate of the attackers we had abandoned in the clearing hanging above us like some dark, malevolent cloud.

I knew my decision made no sense to Robert, but it made perfect sense to me, and it seemed Sir John understood it as well. How could I have slaughtered three men in cold blood, when I already had achieved my aim of disarming them? I could not have had that on my conscience, whatever harm they had planned for us. So I was disappointed in Robert, that he saw a different course of action.

Disappointed, but not altogether surprised.

Now I thought on it, there had been a number of occasions over the past days when he had displayed such poor judgement; occasions such as hiding when his father was being attacked, or when he nearly took me forcibly on the bed in Harwich. Maybe this was more the truth of his character, rather than the occasional moments he showed of inspiration and affection?

This truly mattered. Now we were close to finishing our journey, I knew I had to decide what course my life would take from here. Should I say 'yes' and become the next Lady Fitzwilliam, or say 'no' and see where my fortune would take me otherwise?

---0---

The evening sun was lengthening the shadows across the Suffolk countryside as we came to the end of a narrow lane and halted outside some impressive gates set into a red brick wall.

"Nacton Hall!" announced Sir John. "Our journey's end!"

A servant appeared at the gates and opened them, so we three could ride through.

"Sir John!" he cried. "And Master Robert. You have returned!"

"Aye, Simon," said Sir John, "and we have found the Broken Sword!"

"Heaven be praised!" the man answered. "The mistress and Margaret will be so pleased you are back!"

I could not help but smile at this servant's enthusiasm, and for a few minutes, while we rode up to the impressive manor house, I forgot my dilemma and allowed myself the pleasure of rejoicing in the success of our mission.

A few minutes later we stepped into a large hallway lined with rich tapestries and pictures of smiling ancestors, with an impressive stairway descending to its centre.

"We have made it home – all three whole and hearty, and with this as well!" Sir John fished in his bag and held the Broken Sword triumphantly aloft. "Our mission has been a great success! Yes, we have endured villains a-plenty, been chased many times, been dragged behind a horse, held in a dungeon, had some truly stomach-churning sea voyages – and that is just my part of the tale – but here we are!" He put the Broken Sword back in his bag and turned to me. "And it is thanks in no small part, to the efforts of this wonderful girl before me, Mary Fox!"

"It was naught," I muttered, studying my feet. "I only did what needed to be done."

"Aye, that is true!" he answered. "But I warrant that no other young woman in the Kingdom would – or could – have done the same!"

At that moment, a pretty girl of about fourteen years appeared at the top of the stairs and gave a great cry of joy, then ran down and flung her arms about Sir John's neck, smothering him with kisses.

"Papa!" she cried, once she seemed to have kissed every part of his face. "You are returned!"

"Margaret!" he exclaimed. "How I have missed you!" Then he held her at arm's length, studying her face carefully. "Art fully recovered?"

"Nearly, Papa, nearly. I started to feel better just over a week ago, and every day I have been getting stronger."

Sir John turned to me. "That was when we first found the

Broken Sword! I said, did I not, that having it in my possession would start the curse lifting!"

"But…" Margaret continued, biting her lip, "Mama is still not her old self."

"Mama?" asked Robert, stepping forward so his sister could see him. "She is not recovered also?"

"Robert!" Margaret cried. She ran to him and gave him as many kisses, then she stood back and said, "No, she still ails, and she has not eaten this many a day. I fear for her. We have tried all we can to get her to eat, but she says she cannot." She turned to Sir John. "Do you have the Broken Sword with you, Papa? Please say you do, for that will help Mama so much."

Sir John reached into his bag and took out the talisman once more. "See, Pumpkin, I have it here."

Margaret gave another great cry, then she grabbed it and ran through a pair of double doors to one side of the stairs. We followed her into what was clearly the Great Hall, to see her jump onto the high table. She reached up and put the Broken Sword into a small recess on the wall, that looked as if it was there for the very purpose of displaying the piece.

"There, Papa, it is back!" She jumped down and surveyed it with a nod. Then she said, "Come, let us go up to Mama and give her the good tidings!"

We followed her out of the hall and up the stairs, where she led us into a bedchamber. Running up to the bed, she leaned through the drapes and said, "Mama! Mama! Papa and Robert are home! And they have returned the Broken Sword!"

The men went up to the bed and leaned in. I could hear them talking but could not see the woman inside. I hung back, not wishing to intrude on their reunion, but after a minute or two, I noticed that Margaret had stepped away from the bed and was now observing me with a frown.

"Who are you?" she asked.

"My name is Mary Fox."

"Yes, but who are you?"

"I have helped your father and Robert return here with the Broken Sword."

She looked me up and down. "Why are you dressed as a boy?"

I smiled. "It is quite a long story."

"Oh." The frown disappeared, to be replaced by the sunny smile which I guessed was her more normal disposition. "Then we shall walk together shortly, and you can tell me all."

After a moment Sir John came over. "I see you have met Mary," he said to Margaret. "Without her we would not be here, and nor would the Broken Sword."

Margaret's smile broadened, "Mary is to tell me all!"

Sir John nodded. "Indeed, but before that, I would like her to meet my wife." He beckoned me forward, and I parted the drapes and leaned into the bed. A pale, sickly-looking woman was sitting up against the bolster. She had her hair in a simple cotton coif, and I could see she was a handsome woman, for all she was not well. Sir John said, "Anne, I would like to introduce Mary Fox. She is a brave, resourceful and loving young woman, who saved my life on the day we first met, then did all in her power to help us return the Broken Sword to its rightful place."

Anne Fitzwilliam gave me a small smile. "I am forever in your debt, Mistress Fox," she murmured. She pushed herself a little higher on the bolster. "And I understand you were successful."

I nodded. "Indeed, Lady Fitzwilliam, the Broken Sword is now back in its place in the Great Hall."

"How wonderful." She looked at Sir John. "Indeed, I would like to see it in its place, myself." She paused, looking at both of us in turn. Then she pushed herself higher still and said, "I think I may come down and take some small supper this evening."

---O---

Sir John, Robert, Margaret and I took our places for supper at the table in the Great Hall, and a few minutes later Lady Fitzwilliam came in slowly, still in her nightdress, and sat between her husband and her son.

I was sitting next to Margaret, who had taken me very much under her charge and was now treating me as her life-long friend.

The evening had started with her insisting we should try on as many gowns as she had in her chamber, and, not wishing to offend at this early stage, I had allowed her to parade me in a variety of garments, to brush my hair for many minutes, and even to experiment with a little rouge on my cheeks and lips.

When she had reached what she considered to be the desired result, we had walked together in the grounds and it was easy to fall under the spell of her infectious enthusiasm. She had demanded then that I tell her my full story.

"Oh, you poor girl!" she cried, as I told of my stepfather

and his plans for my marriage. When I came to the part involving the well at Marchington Manor, she gasped and went white, saying, "I swear I could never do that! You are so brave!" But then, when I told her of Robert's proposal, she positively danced for joy.

"You must marry him!" she cried as she skipped around me. "You must, you must, you must!"

"I told him I would think on it," I answered.

She grasped my hands and gave me an impassioned stare. "You must say yes," she said, suddenly serious. "For then we will be sisters, and I would love you so much to be my sister!" She pulled me towards the house. "Come, we must tell Mama! She will be so pleased; I swear this will make her well again in an instant!"

I was dragged back into Lady Fitzwilliam's chamber.

"Mama!" Margaret cried, throwing aside the drapes, "I have the very best news!" She took her mother's thin hand and kissed it. "Mama, Robert has asked Mary Fox to be his wife! Is that not the best thing possible? Robert shall have a wife, and I shall have a sister!"

Lady Fitzwilliam leaned forward. "Is this true, Mary?"

"It is true that he has asked, although I have not yet agreed."

"Why so?" asked Margaret, stamping her foot. "He is quite the catch, is he not, my brother?"

"Shush, Margaret," said her mother. "You must not put Mary under such pressure." She turned to me. "John has told me briefly about your life in Essex, and your dreadful step-father." She considered me a moment, a thin smile on her face. "You will be most welcome to call this family your own, my child." She paused. "And here you will be free to do, and to dress, as you please."

"That is so kind, Lady Fitzwilliam…" I began

"You must call me Anne," she interrupted. "I care not for ceremony."

"Thank you… Anne," I answered, and suddenly I felt as if a great weight had been lifted off me, for now I realised I had what I had truly desired!

To have a warm, loving family, with no expectations of dress and behaviour! To have the vivacious young Margaret as a sister. To have Anne, God willing she recovered fully, as a mother, and to have the kind Sir John as a loving father!

If I had imagined such an outcome the day I had packed Hestia's saddlebags and stolen away from Marchington Manor, I could not have imagined a better one than this.

And yet…

There was one part of this that did not fit with my expectations. For the only way to achieve this blissful family state would be – to marry Robert.

And once he was my husband, it would be Robert who decided all aspects of my life, not his mother and father. In law, he would hold total sway over such decisions as the clothes I wore, and how I behaved.

I would go from being my stepfather's property, to becoming Robert's.

"What ails you, my child?" asked Anne, leaning forward. "You had a sunny look of happiness just now, but it has become all clouded over."

I paused a moment. "You create a warm and loving picture – and one I had always dreamed of." I said. "But I fear that as my husband, it will be Robert's view of our life together that counts. And I know his view to be a little more… restricted."

"Then I shall speak to him," she said, and a small red flush crept into her pale cheeks. "He will need to learn to be more understanding, like his father." She lay back on the bolster. "And now I need to sleep, if I am to have the strength to join you at supper."

---O---

Once Anne had seated herself next to her son at the table, I noted how she turned to him and started a conversation in low tones. At first it appeared very amiable, but soon it seemed that she was admonishing him, and from the side-long glances that both made in my direction, I concluded that I was their subject. As a diversion I tried to be engaged by Margaret's giggling observations, and by the fine foods being placed before us – but in truth, I was much more interested in Robert and Anne.

Then something occurred which took everyone's attention.

Simon, the servant who had first let us in at the gate, came into the hall and whispered something to Sir John. His master nodded, and Simon went out, returning shortly with a grizzled older man in the traveling clothes of a high-ranking nobleman.

Sir John stood. "My lord, you are most welcome as always. Please," he indicated a space at the table, "sit and take food with us. My home is yours."

The nobleman bowed, swept off his cap, and said, "I thank

you, Sir John, but I am bidden to Court at Richmond, so I must continue my journey. I wanted only to give you some good tidings in person as I was passing."

"Good tidings, my lord?" asked Anne.

"Indeed, Lady Fitzwilliam." He replaced his cap, then accepted a goblet of wine offered by Simon and took a sip. "I have lately come from Norwich," he began, "where I heard that discussions were in place regarding the land enclosure planned for this part of Suffolk. I was party to some conversations with the Duke of Norfolk, who, as you know, was the driving force behind these plans. I enquired what was the purpose behind them, and the extraordinary rents that were also being raised. The Duke's answer did not, I believe, make financial sense, and I concluded he was motivated by some form of petty grievance rather than sound husbanding of the land. So I challenged him most strongly on this, and after a while he bowed to my arguments, as a leaf on a branch bows to the wind." He took another sip of wine, and I could see he was revelling in his tale. "So, I am pleased to tell you, my dear Sir John, that the extraordinary rents are no longer due, and that your lands will not be forfeit for enclosure."

There was a stunned silence for a few moments, then Sir John said slowly, "You mean, my lord, that this threat is lifted?"

"I do."

Sir John looked over to each of us in turn, then back at the nobleman. "I have no words except of the deepest gratitude, sir. You have brought us the best news we could have hoped to hear."

"My pleasure." The man drained his goblet and handed it

back to Simon. "Now I must bid you and your fine family good night and wish you all the best of health and happiness."

With that, he bowed again to Anne, replaced his cap and marched out of the hall.

Again there was a silence.

"What has just occurred?" asked Sir John eventually.

"It was the Broken Sword, Papa," breathed Margaret, pointing up at it. "It has restored my health; Mama is at supper for the first time in many days, and your worries about land and money have now disappeared. It was all the Broken Sword."

"So it seems, Pumpkin, so it seems."

"And," Margaret looked pointedly at me, "Mary Fox is going to marry Robert!"

---O---

Sir John waited until the hubbub had died down and everyone had stopped talking over each other, then he said to me, "Is this true, Mary? Have you agreed to Robert's proposal?"

I bit my lip and gave a small shrug, as I did not want to commit to words what I was feeling at that moment.

The truth was, I did not know.

There was no doubt that in part, I wanted to jump up and scream "Yes, yes! I will marry Robert, because in truth, that is the smallest price to get the loving family I have always wanted!" I could see how I would gain the peace and security that would come from no longer being beholden to my stepfather or being forced to marry Sir Reginald. How I would love the freedom from fear!

Freedom…

But would it be the freedom I truly sought? Or would I simply be changing one servitude for another?

I would become the dutiful wife, and no doubt be expected to produce a succession of sons and daughters, until my body was spent, like an empty bag. That would be if I did not die in childbirth like my own poor mother.

And I would have to dress to impress the acquaintances and friends of my husband.

My husband…

A set of pictures appeared in quick succession before my eyes: Robert relieving himself in the forest; Robert dead drunk in old Tom Reeves's hut; Robert standing in our chamber in Harwich with his hose half-way down his legs… Then the final picture; Robert preparing to run a defenceless Cruddon through with his sword…

Or…

I could carve out my own unique position in society. Become a free spirit, unconstrained by convention, unconstrained by expectations. Be the girl I was born to be.

I stared at Robert and Sir John, then at Anne and Margaret.

It was as if all the uncertainties I had been facing these past few days had suddenly disappeared like morning mist in the wind.

I now knew for certain what I should do.

"No," I said. "No, I am sorry. You have all been so kind, but the answer is no." I studied them each in turn; Robert looking sad but not particularly surprised; Sir John looking shocked; Anne was sorrowful and Margaret close to tears.

"There is so much more I want to do. So much more of the world I want to see." I shook my head. "I accept that is not what you wanted to hear, but I must be true to my destiny." I leaned across and took Robert's hand. "I am not the girl you wanted," I said, looking directly into his eyes. "I will never be the dutiful wife you said you seek – instead, I will be like an unbroken filly that kicks and bites and only wants to run away. You are a good man, Robert, and you deserve a better woman."

I turned to Sir John. "You wanted to return the Broken Sword, and you have succeeded in your mission. Your fortunes and your family have been restored. I shall always feel blessed that I have had a part in making that happen, but I am sorry, my journey has to continue."

To Anne, I said, "Even in less than a day, you have shown me such kindness. I shall never forget that, and I wish you God's speed in your recovery. If I had a mother, I would wish she were exactly as you."

I looked at Margaret. "You will always be my beloved sister," I said. "So please remember me as a sister should, with same fondness and love I bear for you."

All in the room were silent. My determination must have been clear to them, and so was the futility of trying to make me change my mind. Eventually Sir John said, "We shall be forever in your debt, Mary. Go in peace, and remember us kindly, as we shall remember you."

"I will," I said.

---O---

The following afternoon I prepared to take my leave, dressed once again in my boy's jerkin and breeches. It was after a day of somewhat forced jollity and – on the part of Margaret – several attempts to make me change my mind. She had tried various approaches, from a simple appeal to my better instincts, to a long exposition on the finer points of her brother's character. But I had made it clear that my mind was not to be changed, and eventually she accepted that while we might now be sisters, it was always going to be a distant relationship.

Eventually Sir John, Robert and I were standing at the gate.

I was holding the same horse I had arrived on at Nacton Hall, which had once been Jacob Cruddon's. The beast was no Hestia, but as I had formed something of an understanding with him since he had become mine, I hoped he would serve me well on adventures to come.

"Where will you head?" asked Robert in a flat voice.

"I have a mind to go first to Ipswich, then see where my fortune takes me."

Sir John pointed up the lane. "Ipswich is that way. No more than a couple of hours' ride, but it will be dark when you arrive. Do not enter the Red Lion; it is known to be a regular meeting place for scoundrels." He gave a thin smile. "The type of men we sought so unsuccessfully to avoid on our journey from Walton."

"I will be sure to remember that," I answered. I kissed

Robert briefly on the lips. "Farewell, Robert," I said aloud, then I leaned in closer and whispered, "I am glad you were not quite the weed I thought you were to start."

He smiled. "But you will always be Saint Joan to me." Then he took my hand and held it firm. "Fare thee well, Mary Fox," he said. "Enjoy your adventures. And watch your back – for you put yourself once again in danger."

"I know," I said. "I understand I am giving up safety – but I have to do so, whatever fate has in store for me."

After that there was no more to be said. I mounted my horse, wheeled him round and headed up the path in the direction of Ipswich.

20

CHAPTER TWENTY

Sir John was right; it was dark when I arrived in the town, and I rode around for some time looking for an inn for the night. Eventually I saw a small house with lit windows and the sound of laughter coming from within, but when I got closer I saw a sign saying, 'The Red Lion', so I kept riding. A few minutes later I spied another such hostelry and trotted up. This one called itself 'The Green Dragon', so I stabled my horse, and went in.

It certainly felt strange to be entering any sort of tavern alone, especially after these days travelling in the company of Robert and Sir John, and I found myself wondering, as I had many times on the journey to Ipswich, if I had made the right choice. But once again I had the feeling of lead in my belly at the thought of being tied down to Robert in marriage, followed by the wonderful feeling of freedom and release knowing I had refused him. Whatever happened, I was happy in my choice. So I took a deep breath, sat myself at a free table, and ordered a pie and ale.

I was aware of the many stares in my direction as I sat. A woman alone was strange enough, but one wearing a man's jerkin and breeches with hair uncovered caused many a raised eyebrow. These clothes had been not been clean when I had changed into them in the tavern at Walton while we waited for Cruddon. After a forest journey that included rolling on the ground under a carriage and a sword fight, for sure they were not looking their best. Would I be arrested and held as a vagrant? That could be a real possibility, so I ate my pie and drank my ale as fast as possible, before requesting a room and locking myself in for the night.

As I broke fast the next morning, I decided a change of clothing would be necessary; something that would let me not stand out as a vagrant, but not be too restrictive so I could still move with ease.

I decide to ask the way to the market, intending to seek out a clothier. The first person I approached was a grey-bearded old man, but he took one look at me and scuttled away like a frightened crab. The next person was a matronly woman out walking with her husband, who told me there was no market this day, but fortunately was prepared to direct me to a street where there were some stores selling clothing.

I selected a simple serving girl's dress in green with a white apron and a white cotton coif for my head. I thought that if challenged, I could say I was in service, travelling about my master's business. Pleased with this, I walked back to the Green Dragon, to collect my horse.

As I walked, I took stock of the situation I had put myself into when I had ridden from Nacton Hall.

On the positive side, I had successfully made myself free of Marchington Manor, and was unconstrained by any restrictive stepfather or unwelcome marriage – to either Sir Reginald or Robert. I was able to go where I wished, wear what I wished, and do as I pleased. So far, so good.

On the negative side, I was a woman alone on the road, and technically homeless. I could be arrested at any time as a vagrant, or accused of witchcraft, or attacked by any man fancying his chances. Vagrancy was realistically only a risk if I had to beg for alms, for the laws were aimed at those who could not pay their way. The reassuring weight of the purses at my belt suggested that I should be able to counter such a charge.

Witchcraft was a concern. As a woman alone, without a man to be her protector, I would be vulnerable to even a casual accusation. But such accusations were mostly to blame a local woman for some misfortune, so I vowed always to try and be the cause of good. That way I would be less likely to draw such attention.

Then there was attack by a man, or men, seeking to rape me. Well, for that I had the sword hidden beneath my skirt, a quick pair of feet, and a wary eye for danger. I resolved to keep to the shadows, avoid drawing attention, and always have an escape route.

Which is advice I should have recalled, as I entered the stables to make ready my horse.

As I patted the beast's muzzle, fed him some oats and

water then saddled him up, I was not aware of the stable door opening and a man coming in, until suddenly my hands were grabbed and pulled roughly behind my back.

"What the…!" was all I could say, before a filthy rag was put in my mouth and bound behind my head, as my hands were also tied together.

The unseen assailant pulled the cords painfully tight so they were cutting into my wrists, then spun me round so I faced him.

It was Tobias Whyte, my would-be rescuer from the hotel in Harwich.

Only now he was my attacker, whistling carelessly as he lifted my skirt, removed my sword and both purses, then attached them to his own belt.

"We meet again, Mistress Mary Fox," he said with a twisted smile. "I was told to expect resistance, but it seems the element of surprise made it all too easy."

The man was no heavier than me, and barely any taller, so it galled me greatly that I had not been able to resist him. I tried to aim a kick at his shins in their expensive boots, but he stepped smartly away, and I nearly overbalanced.

"Come now," he laughed, "let us not be rash." He drew my own sword and held it against my side. "I say we step outside, eh, Mary. What say you?" He gestured me to leave the stable. I gave him my foulest stare but did as he said.

We emerged into the yard, with him pushing me forward at sword-point, and headed towards a box-cart that looked similar to the one used by the original brigand back in the Essex forest. It was made of rough timber with solid wooden wheels and had a seat on the front for the driver.

A man was standing beside it, holding a chestnut horse with a white blaze like an arrow pointing down its face.

I would have recognised that gaunt, hateful figure anywhere.

It was Sir Reginald.

I cursed my fate. I could have stayed in safety at Nacton Hall. But now I had no choice but to accept the consequences of my decision to leave…

"You are well met, Mary," he said with a cold smile as I approached. "You have led us on a merry chase indeed, since the night when you retrieved that old hilt from the well at Marchington Manor." He raised an eyebrow. "How did you manage that? Did you use the rope we found to descend into the depths yourself, and so avoid turning the broken capstan?" I nodded slightly, and his eyes widened. "Truly remarkable! I would not have believed it possible."

He shook his head. "The boat to Harwich – disembarking before she reached the harbour where we waited." He gave a low chuckle. "Then trying to deny your own name and leaving me to my fate with Tobias here and his companions – although with good fortune, they were able to see the truth of your wilful behaviour, and join my cause."

He whistled softly. "Then the trick with the merchant and his wife and servant to fool us at the docks – you are quite the little schemer!"

I could hardly tell him that the plan was not mine, with a filthy rag in my mouth.

"Then leaping aboard that boat to the far shore. If those boys had told us a moment sooner that they had spotted you, we would have caught you, but no, you slipped away from us once again."

He paused. "Do you know, we then followed you all the way from Walton? At first we thought we had missed you, but we spotted you riding off in some perilous old carriage, so we were able to follow at a distance." He paused, looking at me coldly, his earlier forced jollity gone. "We thought we might have lost you again, once you went into the dark forest, but then we observed you had stopped, and were fighting with that old fellow in a clearing."

He nodded. "Nice sword-play, Mary, I will give you that. We were some way back, but I could see you defended well, blocking each move he made. Then you went on the offensive, and I will admit, despite myself, I was impressed." He stepped closer, looking down on me from his height. "I thought – that girl who fights well, she will be my wife. She has resisted me, she has made me look a fool, she has denied her own name, but she has fire and she has passion. So when she is my wife, I will use that. I will have fun with that, when we are alone in our chamber."

If my hatred were a sword I would have impaled him with my eyes.

"Yes," he continued, seeming to ignore this, "I was im-pressed. Although I would have been more so, had you run the fellow through, as your ineffectual-looking companion seemed so keen to do. But nay, the fellow had tripped up and knocked himself out, so you left him to his fate instead. Most generous of you, Mary. Although we slung his carcass over a horse and brought him here to Ipswich, where it seems he has his home." He gave a mirthless chuckle. "The one-eyed old fellow has a solid head, for by the time we arrived he had recovered, and he has vowed revenge on you. It seems you have made a habit of attacking his family, and he feels this should not go unpunished. But I told him you were my betrothed, and I would have you under my protection." Again, he gave a dry laugh. "So it seems I am to be a loving and generous husband, protecting you from such enemies that you have collected on your adventures."

He opened the small door at the back of the box-cart as Tobias moved behind me. I felt my hands being unbound and the gag was removed.

"Damn you, de Courtney," I growled. "I will never consent to be your wife."

"I care not what you say," he replied. "If your father and I say you will be wed, then you will be wed. I believe he advised you that his alternative is a little more… permanent?" He nodded. "So now we return to Essex and thence to our happy marriage vows. But I cannot risk you escaping through your trickery yet again, so I would have Tobias here drive you in this cart." He nodded with a sick smile. "It is fitting, is it not? On the day you first ran from your father and your home, you gave us to think you were hiding in such a cart as this. We lost many minutes as we forced the door open, only to find your torn-off sleeves."

I felt myself being pushed towards the cart by the point of my sword, and had no option but to climb in. I crawled round and looked back at the bright sunlight, as Sir Reginald stared inside.

"So this time, when we open the cart at Marchington Manor, you will be there in person, ready to beg your father's forgiveness and prepared to become my wife." He looked up at Tobias, who must have climbed onto the driver's seat. "I have some other business to attend to here. I will see you at the Sun Inn at Dedham as we discussed."

He looked back at me, trapped in his infernal cart like a dog in a kennel. He laughed. "I wish you a pleasant journey, Mary Fox!"

With that he slammed the door and I heard it being secured.

Then I was alone in total darkness.

21

CHAPTER TWENTY-ONE

The box cart jolted and crunched as it made its way along, throwing me bodily from side to side so I had to put my hands to the walls to avoid being knocked senseless.

Gradually I became used to the darkness and started to make out the dim interior by the sliver of light coming through the edge of the door.

There was nothing in the cart except for myself; no straw, no water and no food; just me, sitting upright. Carefully, I hit my heel on the boards beneath me, timing it to coincide with a bump in the path so as not to raise the suspicion of Tobias. Unfortunately, these boards were sound with no feel of rottenness, so the chance to repeat my dramatic escape from Cruddon's carriage was not going to happen.

I rested my back against the front wall, to try and get some respite from holding it upright while seated, then quickly moved away again as a particularly bad bump made me fetch a resounding crack on the back of my head.

So then I tried to lie down. I could get to my full length, but every movement of the cart caused me to slide back and forward, causing me to crack the top of my head instead. Reluctantly I sat up, putting my hands out once again to brace myself against the sides of the cart.

As we bumped along, I gradually became aware that there was a regular squeaking noise; a distinctive high-pitched grinding *'screech – screech – screech'* sound that occurred with monotonous regularity on every revolution of one of the wheels. I groaned to myself. Now I had noticed it, I knew that unless I could work out a way to accept it, it would soon become a form of torture.

There were other noises, too – that were irregular and therefore manageable. If I could concentrate on those, maybe I could ignore the regular squeak? That occasional creaking of the timbers, perhaps? Or the thump as one of the wheels crashed into a dip in the path? These were noises I could listen out for, so taking my mind off the annoyance of the regular sound…

Screech. Screech. Screech.

I tried to put my hands over my ears, but that meant I was once again thrown around the inside of the cart like a pea in a drum, so I quickly put them back out again.

Screech. Screech. Screech.

It was going to be a long journey.

We had been in Ipswich when we set off, and Sir Reginald

had mentioned meeting us at Dedham. I tried to imagine the maps I had once seen of Suffolk and Essex, to try and make a calculation as to how long this hellish journey would take. It was around ten or twelve miles to Dedham, then maybe another thirty or so to Maldon. We would be travelling at the pace of a walking horse, so would take maybe three hours to Dedham. Thence it would perhaps be a day and a half to Marchington Manor.

Allowing for night-time stops, that would be at least two days and a night.

A particularly bad jolt sent me sprawling, once again hitting my head on the side as I went down.

I resolved two things.

First, that I must continue to position myself so I could absorb every movement of the bumpy cart, or I would be slumped in concussion when they finally opened the door. I settled myself in the middle of the cart and again put my hands to the walls beside me to maintain my balance. They were rough wood, and I felt sure I would be stuck like a pin cushion with splinters before long. Then I permitted myself a wry chuckle. At least that would be preferable to being knocked senseless!

I moved my hands higher and found a rough wooden ledge running all round, a few inches below the roof. I gripped it tightly and flexed my arms ready for the next jolt.

Screech. Screech. Screech.

The second thing I resolved, was that somehow, I would escape.

The light in the cart grew a bit brighter, or maybe my eyes

were more used to it, so now I could clearly make out the space I was in. It was maybe seven feet in length and half that in width, and as I had seen initially, was empty save for myself. But that gave me hope – for if there was no food placed inside for a journey of two days and a night, then they would have to feed me. For all his evil ways, I did not think Sir Reginald would countenance me arriving in a state of weak starvation.

No, he would want me to be at least fed meagre rations – which would mean opening the door, even if for a second to throw food inside.

And if the door opened, then I had a chance.

As the cart jolted along, I started to make my plans.

Screech. Screech. Screech.

---0---

It was a couple of hellish hours later that I felt the cart come to a stop.

A blessed stillness settled on my dismal little world, and I let my arms drop to my side with a small cry of relief. As I massaged my forearms to try and restore feeling, I felt the cart rock as the driver dropped to the ground and heard his footsteps crunching on the path, heading away from the cart. Then there was a sound of falling liquid, and I guessed he was relieving himself.

The footsteps headed back, and I heard the voice of Tobias from outside.

"We will be arriving in Dedham soon," he said, and I could hear the sickly smile in his tone.

"Are you going to let me out?" I asked. There was a long pause, and I nearly repeated the question.

"Nay," he replied. "You will stay in there."

"I need to piss," I said. "You would leave a girl to piss in this cage?"

"Aye," he said, "I would."

"You once tried to save me, Tobias," I said. "Yet now you tell me to soil myself?"

"I have my instructions."

"You listen to me...," I began, but he interrupted.

"No, you listen to me, Mary Fox! You are a sorry liar, that would run from an honourable man who is contracted to you in marriage, and who would cherish and keep you well. Sir Reginald desires only to end the unnatural behaviour that so ill befits a woman of your standing, so I say he is cruelly wronged. I am only helping to right that wrong." There was another long pause, then he said, "So I will not hear any of your lies or weasel words, lest you try and turn my head."

"It is not I who has turned your head," I said. "It is Sir Reginald."

"Aye, and he said you would try such trickery," he answered. "So I shall ignore it." There was another pause, then he added, "I am charged with bringing you to Marchington Manor, and that I will do."

"Am I to eat?" I asked.

"Later," he said. "Some bread when we get to Dedham. That is all."

There was the sound of his steps crunching round to the

front of the cart, then it rocked again as he mounted the driver's seat.

I raised my sore arms to their station once more, as the cart lurched forward, and again I braced myself against the relentless bumps and crashes caused by the road.

As we made our slow way, I could not help but think that it was a sorry state of affairs, that had brought me to the dark inside of this little cart. How full of hope I had been, when I first rode away from Marchington all those days ago! How easy had it been to fall in with Sir John and Robert, blissfully unaware that this decision would cause such hardship. Had I but known that I would end up being lowered headfirst down a stinking black well, that I would escape my stepfather by seconds through the gate, be attacked on Hythe Quay, almost be thrown overboard from the *Curliewe*, then escape Sir Reginald in the tavern, only to have to resist Robert in the bed chamber, then fight Cruddon in the forest... For sure, I would have pursued a different path.

But then, I would not have helped Sir John and his family restore their heath, wealth and happiness by returning the Broken Sword. I would have not met Robert and experienced the intrigue of being loved by another. I would not have learned better how to create and execute a plan of action. Or to be the leader of men; the person looked to by others for direction – no, on balance, perhaps the hardship was worth it, for all I had learned things that perhaps helped me to be a better person.

A sudden jolt of the cart threw my head hard against the side. As stars lit up the darkness, it brought me back to the unpleasant reality of my little prison and the imminent return to Marchington Manor. And with that, the living death of being married to Sir Reginald.

Or the alternative – my very real death at the hands of my stepfather.

Now was the time to plan my escape.

And for that, I had formed an idea.

22

CHAPTER TWENTY-TWO

It was probably no more than half an hour later, although it did seem longer, when we stopped again.

If Tobias were to be believed, now would be the time when he would open the cart to give me food.

As the door opened, I was ready.

Tobias's head appeared silhouetted against the bright sky, as he peered into the cart.

"I have bread…" He paused. "By heaven," he muttered, "she has disappeared!"

His head moved deeper into the cart, looking left and right. "Mary? Mary? By Christ, where art…?"

Then he looked up, but it was too late.

I dropped down onto him from above, where I had suspended myself using the ledge running round near the roof as a support. As I came down, I brought my fists together and used all my force to knock his head onto the floor of the cart.

He gave a grunt and slumped as I landed on top of him.

I crawled past him out of the cart and flopped onto the cobblestones next to his feet. I took a moment to catch my breath, then stood and checked his wrist. There was a reasonable pulse, so I knew he still lived.

I took in my surroundings. The cart was standing in a courtyard with stables on one side and a wood-beamed building on the other. Anyone could walk past or observe from inside, so I needed a more secluded place for the next part of my plan.

I slid Tobias fully out of the cart and grabbed him under his shoulders. Quickly I dragged him over to an open stable with his boots bumping across the cobbles. Once inside I laid him out on the straw.

After reassuring myself again that he still had a pulse, I closed the stable door and proceeded to disrobe him. Then, once he was down to his cotton shirt and nothing else, I pulled off my green servant's dress and eventually managed to get it onto him, with much struggling and cursing on my part, while he stayed thankfully asleep. I then dressed myself in his hose, nether stocks, doublet, boots and hat, which I pulled down low over my face. Once my sword and purses were restored to my belt, as well a small dagger I found on him, I permitted myself a small sigh of relief. I was now a passable presentation of Tobias Whyte, and he, sitting slumped against the stable wall in my dress and slippers, with his long hair secured under my cotton coif, could easily be taken for me.

So far, my plan was going well. It had been born out of the observation that Tobias was of a similar build to me, if a little taller, and had hair of a colour and length that seemed to match mine. I smiled to myself. Had he been a foot taller and as broad as most men, then I would have had to think differently, but as it was, my plans allowed for the sleeping figure in the green dress to pass as me.

There was a halter rope hanging from a hook, which I cut into two parts. One I used to bind his hands behind his back; the other I tied about his head and in his mouth as a gag. It was fitting, I thought as I tightened the knots, that I was now tying and gagging him, where it been he who had done me the same service in Ipswich.

There was a little water in the horse-trough, so I cupped it in my hands and threw it on his face. After a few moments, his eyes opened and focussed slowly on me. Then he tried to speak and realised he was gagged, before trying to move his hands and finding they were tied. Then he looked down at his legs and could see them covered in my green servant's dress.

His eyes narrowed and he shook his head, as if to say 'you will not get away with this!'

I ignored such an empty threat, as I prepared the next part of my plan.

I picked up the dagger, which I decided was easier to manage than the sword and pushed it into the soft part of his side, just below his ribs. "Get up," I ordered.

He stared at me with a look that suggested defiant hatred. "I said, get up," I repeated, pushing the dagger in just enough to draw a wince of pain and a spot of blood to appear on the green cloth. Slowly he staggered to his feet, swaying slightly, then fell back against the stable wall, no doubt still suffering the effects of his lack of consciousness.

He stared at me some more, and I was about to let him have a minute to recover fully, when I noticed a small but regular movement in his shoulders and arms.

"No, you do not," I ordered and reapplied the dagger, making him move away from the wall to reveal a small nail sticking out of the boards that he had been trying to use to fray the ropes about his wrists. "Stand away from the wall and that nail."

If a man can snarl with a piece of dirty horse rope in his mouth, then Tobias Whyte snarled at me. "Come," I said, moving round and pushing the dagger between his shoulder blades, "walk to the cart and get in."

This he did with a singular lack of grace, somewhat out of keeping with the womanly figure he presented. Once inside, he stayed facing the front and presented his bound hands to me.

"Nay," I said, "you must stay bound and gagged."

He shuffled round and stared with pleading eyes. "Nay," I repeated. "I am not going to change my mind."

His eyes narrowed once more in hatred, as I closed the door and secured it, then climbed up to the driver's seat.

I tried hard to feel sorry for Tobias Whyte, but I must confess, I found it most difficult. True, the man had tried to rescue me when the worse for drink – but thereafter he had shown himself no saviour of mine. Believing the lies fed to him by Sir Reginald, he had stood watch on the house where we had lodged, then attacked me in a stable and condemned me to a tortuous journey in a cramped space, with no food and no chance to take a piss, although it should be said, my request at the time was motivated by more of a desire to escape than actual need.

My need now was for food, as a long low rumble came from under my doublet.

I looked over at the building next to me. It had a sign fixed to the jutting upper floor by a stout metal bar, swinging in the gentle breeze, that announced it was The Sun Inn. So this was the place where Sir Reginald had said he would meet Tobias.

I looked at the stables. None of the horses I could see had the distinctive arrow blaze on its nose that would mark it as Sir Reginald's, so I took it that he had not yet arrived.

I looked back at the Sun Inn. I could perhaps be in and out in no more than half an hour. But could I risk not being in the driver's seat when Sir Reginald did arrive? My disguise might fool him if I were already seated with my head down, but would it fool him if he saw me walk from the inn? My gait was that of a girl, however I might try to swagger like a man, and my beardless chin would mark me if I lifted my head.

Another rumble followed the first. This one was longer and louder, followed by a cramping hunger pain. With a small prayer, I jumped down and went into the Sun Inn.

It was a small coaching inn, with a single room for food and drink that featured a vaulted roof with elaborate oaken beams, plus a balustraded stair, no doubt heading up to bedchambers where the weary traveller could lay down for the night.

Keeping my head low I found a table with a view of the cart through an open window and ordered a pie and some ale.

As I waited for these, I kept glancing out, but the cart sat undisturbed and there was no sign of Sir Reginald.

The food and drink arrived, and I ate with speed and a marked lack of grace. How refreshing it was not to be bound by the restrictions of my sex, able to quaff the ale heartily and shovel pie into my mouth with such abandon! I even permitted myself a small belch, just to show any casual observer what a jolly chap I was.

As I stood to leave, I heard a sound that, even though it was expected, still made my blood turn to ice in my veins.

It was the sound of three horsemen clattering into the courtyard and coming to a halt, with much neighing from the horses and steam rising from their flanks.

Cautiously I peered out. As I thought, it was Sir Reginald de Courtney and two of his men.

I decided to walk out while they were dismounting, so perhaps they would not be paying full attention. Pausing only to smear some beef dripping from the remains of the pie onto my chin in a crude and somewhat desperate approximation of Tobias's beard, I sauntered out and walked over to the cart.

"Whyte?" called Sir Reginald. I stopped at the side of the cart and glanced up at him from under my cap.

"Aye?" I growled, making my voice as deep as I could.

He stared at me with a look that went on a little too long for my comfort.

Then he said, "Have you eaten?"

"Aye."

"And the girl?"

"Aye."

I noticed something lying by the back wheel.

It was hard to see what it was at first, but then I made it out. It had the look of a small piece of rock, all brown and rough. Then I decided it was not a rock but looked more like a piece of bread.

Bread!

I swallowed hard. It must have been the food Tobias had brought for me when I ambushed him. It had fallen to the ground and I had not seen it till now.

If Sir Reginald noticed it, it would give the lie to what I had just said, and his undoubted suspicions would grow.

Before he could follow my gaze, I turned and climbed quickly up to the driver's seat, then pulled back hard on the reins, while making as if to settle the horse. Thankfully the beast responded, moving back a few steps, and I hoped, making the solid wooden wheel block Sir Reginald's view of the bread.

I continued to make reassuring noises to the horse, mainly to avoid looking at him, while willing him to go into the inn. Then one of his men said, "Come, let us get some food and drink.

I am famished."

There was an uncomfortable pause, then I heard him say, "For sure, for sure. Stay here Whyte. We will be out when we have supped."

"Aye."

He walked away across the cobbles, then his footsteps stopped.

"Have you lost the power of speech, Whyte?" he asked. "That you say only 'aye'?"

"Nay," I responded.

"Hmm," he growled, then went inside.

23

CHAPTER TWENTY-THREE

As Sir Reginald and his men went into the inn, I prepared to execute the next part of my plan.

First I took the opportunity to collect the piece of bread from the cobbles, then I carefully unlocked the door at the back of the cart. Once my eyes became accustomed to the dim light, I could see Tobias slumped dejectedly at the back, still clad in my green dress, with my cotton coif in place on his head.

"You look the part," I observed. "Quite the young maid."

I could just make out his eyes, and they glowered at me with an intensity that should have given me fright, had he not been securely bound and gagged.

"Turn round," I ordered, taking out the dagger.

He shook his head.

"Turn round," I repeated. Then I held up the bread. "If you would rather I did not let you eat…"

He shuffled round and I checked his hands were still securely bound, then undid the gag behind his head.

He shuffled back again and sat in the same position as before, with his legs towards me.

I pushed the knife again into his side. "I shall let you eat this bread and have a drink from this costrel," I told him, "but shout or play me false, and I will split you open with this knife."

He went white as I leaned in and held the bread to his mouth so he could take a bite.

"You would do that to me?" he spluttered as he ate.

"Aye, I would," I answered, trying to sound like the kind of woman who would kill a defenceless man. He swallowed hard, and if anything, went whiter still. I held the rest of the bread to his mouth, and he finished it up. I held up the costrel and let him have a drink of ale.

"Good," I said. "Turn round again." I replaced the gag. "I will be back presently." I paused. "But if I hear any noise from in here…" I tested the edge of dagger with my finger, "I will be back quicker still." With that I gave what I hoped to be an evil-sounding chuckle, then closed and secured the door, leaving him wide-eyed and very still.

In truth, I had no intention of ever coming back to him, but he could not know that. I trusted that the fear of what I might do with the dagger would keep him still and allow me to make good my escape – for that was what I intended now.

Checking that I was not observed by Sir Reginald or his

men through a window, I left the cart and ran back to the empty stable where I had exchanged clothing with Tobias. There I prepared to wait until they came out, and see if my plan would work.

I did not have to wait too long. They marched out of the inn, and Sir Reginald went straight over to the cart.

"By heavens!" he said, looking up at the empty seat. "Where is Whyte?"

"He was acting most strangely before," observed one of the men.

"Aye, that he was." Sir Reginald looked around the cart. "Has he left us completely?"

"Belike he is relieving himself and will be back presently?" suggested the other man.

Sir Reginald said nothing, but went to the back of the cart and undid the lock.

I held on tight to the stable door as I peered over, conscious that sweat was starting to run down my back. Now was the truest test of my plan. Would Sir Reginald be fooled by Tobias, as I had hoped he would be? Or would Tobias be emboldened by the sight of someone looking in that was not me with the knife, and make some movement to show who he really was? I could scarce bear to watch, as Sir Reginald looked in for what seemed like an age, but in truth cannot have been more than the briefest moment.

Finally, he slammed the door, locked it and went over to where his men were standing.

"The woman is still in there," he said, "although it was dark, I could see her form."

I slowly let out my breath, unaware I must have been holding it.

"If Whyte is not here very soon, we will leave without him," Sir Reginald continued. "He will need to make his own way back, and good riddance I say. Weaselly little fellow."

They paced around for another few minutes, then Sir Reginald seemed to make up his mind.

"Right," he said, "we leave without him. Tom, you drive the cart. Hal, you tether Tom's horse to yours. We ride out now."

I watched over the top of the stable door as they made their preparations and eventually rode out of the courtyard. The cart followed with Whyte safely inside; the familiar 'screech, screech, screech' sound of the axle fading into the distance, as it passed under some low branches and finally disappeared round a bend at the bottom of the lane.

They had gone! My plan had worked!

I sat back against the stable wall, and felt the tension of the last few days start to flow out of every muscle in my body. For the first time since I had crept out of Marchington Manor that fateful morning with such hope in my heart, and even when Lady Fitzwilliam had made me the offer of becoming part of the family, I felt finally free.

Free!

Free of my stepfather, who would marry me off to that dreadful man or kill me for refusing. Free of Sir Reginald himself, who would use me so cruelly as his wife. And even free of Robert, who would have made me into the very woman that I would not wish to become.

Free!

I slipped down the wall until I was lying fully on the floor, then in a sudden fit of joy, I waved my arms and legs in and out until I had opened up wings like an angel in the straw, just as my brothers and I had done so often in the winter snow when we were small. Then I drummed my feet on the floor and yelled, "Yes! Yes!"

Eventually the moment passed. I lay in silence a few minutes, listening to my breathing and feeling my heartbeat start to slow, but mainly enjoying the stillness and calm of the stable.

Eventually I stood up, brushed off the straw, practiced a little manly swagger, then made my way into once more into the inn.

The room was full of rowdy travellers eating, drinking and making merry, but luckily the table where I had previously supped was still free. I sat once again and decided I would allow myself a glass of wine in celebration of my freedom. A serving girl came past the table. I requested a cup of Rhenish in as deep a voice as I could muster, while keeping my head down and my cap low. Fortunately the noise of the room was such that she made no question over the pitch of my voice, which still sounded most unmanly to me.

I sat back and gazed about.

It was not a particularly large room – I had seen many inns and taverns that were larger – but it was well-made with its oak-vaulted roof. Light came from sconces on the walls and tallow candles on the tables, as well as the fire roaring in the grate at one end. All together it was a homely and warm room, enjoyed by the men supping and drinking at the tables.

As I enjoyed the wine, I turned my attention to the view from the window. The sun was starting to dip below the horizon, sending red beams into the sky, and making the trees stand out black against it.

Suddenly a feeling of deep fatigue overcame me. It may have been the wine, or the relief at being free – or perhaps both – but I knew I needed to lie down, and soon as I could.

I drained the cup and enquired gruffly if there was a room available. It appeared there was, and I soon found myself laid out on a small, hard, horse-hair bed in a room on the first floor.

I put my hands behind my head and stared up at the old wooden beams. Noises could still be heard from the room below, almost as loud as when I had been down the stairs myself. I let out a deep sigh as my ears were assaulted by frequent shouts and roars of laughter, the crashing of tankards onto tables, the scraping of chairs being pushed back and the slamming of doors.

Then I picked out another sound, a gentle creaking noise. I clambered off the bed in curiosity, and peered out of the open window. It was the Sun Inn name sign swinging on its metal pole, secured to the wall just below me. Beyond it I could see light spilling out into the night from the front door of the building, tucked back under my overhanging room.

Climbing back onto the bed I could see that sleep was clearly out of the question for now. I had no wish to re-join in the merriment below, for there was no doubt my disguise would not have lasted much longer in such boisterous company. And I dreaded to think what such men, made merry with ale, would do if they found they had a single woman in their midst. No, I would stay here abed until there was eventual quiet below, and I could go to sleep.

Then, tomorrow, no doubt there would be some new adventure, as I headed... where?

I bit my lip as I considered my options. I was free to go where I willed – so where should that be?

London? Possibly, although both my stepfather and Sir Reginald had houses there.

The North? It was an option, as neither of them had connections there.

France? Perhaps. It would be good to put water between me and them.

Resolving to give it more thought in the morning, I settled back on the bed and tried to at least make myself comfortable.

Screech. Screech. Screech.

24

CHAPTER TWENTY-FOUR

I swear I screamed aloud as the familiar and hated sound drifted up to my room from the courtyard below.

With my heart thumping fit to burst from my ribs, I crouched by the windowsill, willing it to be some other carriage or cart with the same squeaky axle, but knowing deep inside that the chances of that were slight.

It was indeed my prison cart.

Tobias Whyte was the driver, still clad in my green dress, although the skirts had been roughly cut away to make it more of a tunic, and he had found hose from somewhere. Sir Reginald, Tom and Hal rode alongside.

Tobias brought the cart to a halt, then jumped down as the other men dismounted.

I could imagine how Sir Reginald had once again opened

the back of the cart somewhere on the road to check on his prisoner, but maybe this time with a brazier to light up the interior, and had been confronted with the reality of my deception. From there they would have decided I was likely to have remained at the inn, and had turned back to seek me out.

I saw them share a few words as they tethered their mounts, then stride through the inn door directly below my room.

With a muttered curse I withdrew from the window, buckled on my sword belt and stood a moment thinking what to do. It would be easy for them to enquire if there was a single young man staying in one of the rooms. They would be told that there was indeed, and which room he could be found in. They would then make their way quickly up the stairs.

I pulled the thin blanket from the bed and looked again out of the window. The cobblestone courtyard seemed a long way down. I looked back at the door – it would only be a few moments before they arrived; perhaps they were outside even now.

I pushed the bed across the room so it was hard up against the door – just as the door itself juddered with the pressure of a boot kicking it from outside.

I ran back to the window, leaned out over the sill and tied one end of the blanket to the bar supporting the sign.

It was definitely a long way down; for sure the blanket would only reach part of the way.

The door juddered from another kick.

I looked down again at the cobbles below.

"Mary?" came a shout. "I know you are inside. Come out now and it will go easier on you!"

I took a deep breath, then scrambled up onto the sill. The pole, which had been easily accessible when I had leaned out to tie on the blanket was now much further away when I was standing up.

Gingerly I stepped down onto it, testing my weight with one foot.

It held so I put my other foot down. Carefully I leaned down and grabbed it with one hand. Now I was committed.

Above me I heard another loud kick on the door and the scraping sound of the bed being forced inwards.

I grabbed the pole with the other hand, so I was crouched on top with a hand on either side of my feet. Then I let myself fall backwards, at the same time slipping my feet off, so I was hanging full length, with my nose pressed to the top of the sign itself.

There was a crash from above as the door was finally forced open.

I twisted the blanket about one leg and lowered myself down until I was hanging from the end.

I looked up, to see Sir Reginald's head appear out of the window. I measured the distance to the cobbles, took a deep breath and let myself drop, landing with a bone-jarring crash then rolling forward to absorb the fall.

"Mary!" yelled Sir Reginald, as I ran from the brightly lit doorway into the darkness beyond.

As I ran I heard a sword being drawn just behind me, and spun round to see Sir Reginald's man, the one he called Tom, with his sword out, preparing to lunge.

I had no time to question how he was down here and had not gone up with the others, when he made a sweep that would have removed my head if I had not stepped quickly back.

I drew my own sword and blocked his next move, turning his blade on mine at the last moment, then found myself in a fierce fight as he advanced, his blade thrusting, sweeping and parrying mine.

I soon realised that he had a strong advantage that could cost me the fight. He had the light from the doorway behind him, making him a silhouette with a blade that had no light upon it to make it visible, whereas I and my sword were well-lit to him and easily seen.

So as I fought, one thought was uppermost – how to turn him round so the advantage of the light was with me, while keeping him at bay when I could scarcely see his blade?

My chance came after a particularly vicious lunge which I parried to my right. I used the opportunity to step smartly to the left, forcing him to turn. As he did so I danced round again, so he had to come at me from the other direction, and I now had the advantage of the light behind me. The cart was also a few feet beyond him.

I quickly pressed my advantage, pushing him back towards it with a series of sharp lunges and sweeps of my own, until his back came up against the side of the cart. He was not expecting it to be there, and had a moment of surprise as he hit. This was the opportunity I needed, as for the briefest moment he was distracted. With a flick of my wrist, I sent his sword clattering away across the cobbles, then with another flick across him, I opened his belly with my point.

It was not a mortal wound, but it doubled him over and sent him crashing to the ground clutching at his midriff.

Immediately I turned to see if Sir Reginald, Tobias and the other man Hal were on the scene – and sure enough, they were all emerging from the bright doorway, swords in hand and intent on finishing the task that Tom had started.

I could see that the odds of three to one did not work in my favour across open ground – better for me if I could get inside the inn where there were others to get in the way and re-balance the odds.

I glanced back at the cart and had a sudden idea.

Quickly I climbed up to the driver's seat, grabbed the reins and wheeled the horse round so he was facing the door to the inn. Yelling like a fiend from the depths of Hell, I cracked the reins across his back and urged him forward, straight towards the men advancing on me.

As I moved towards them, they saw they needed to give space to the horse or be trampled beneath his hooves, so they stepped smartly to the sides. As I levelled with them, I stood up and swung my sword both to the left and right, clashing blades with Sir Reginald on one side and Hal on the other, before I was through them and nearly at the door. The horse could see he was not going to fit through, and I felt him pulling up, his ears back and neighing loudly as he scrabbled to stop. As he halted, I sheathed my sword and leapt as lightly as I could onto his hindquarters, then stepped across his back, and vaulted off his withers. As I leapt, I grabbed at the top frame of the door, swung my legs past his neck, then propelled myself feet first into the room like a hawk coming in to land.

The men inside were silenced as I dropped into their midst, all staring at me with their mouths open. But I had no time to worry about their concerns, as I scarce had landed and turned back to the door when Tobias burst in, seemingly from beneath the horse's forelegs. He advanced on me with a sword drawn, an evil grin on his pallid face. I drew my own sword and we faced each other.

"I see you have altered my dress," I observed. "I will not ask for its return."

"That, Mary Fox, is the last joke you will ever make," he growled, and advanced on me, swinging his sword in such wide sweeps that I saw men at the tables on either side of him ducking their heads. "I will show no mercy for the sake of your humour."

As I let him advance a few more steps I heard some men behind me muttering to each other; "Mary? Did he say 'Mary?' By the Lord, 'tis a girl?"

"Aye, now I look on her…"

"Did you see her leap in like an acrobat just now? T'was a wonder to behold…"

"Quiet, fellow. She dresses as a man – let us see if she can fight like one…"

Tobias made some ever wilder swings, proving what I had begun to suspect – that he was no natural swordsman.

"Come now, Tobias," I said, "do not make yourself a fool. Drop your sword and let us forget this nonsense."

"No." He paused his swinging and pointed his blade at me. "You bound and gagged me, you dressed me as a woman and threatened to kill me; that is not something I am like to forget."

At this several of the men sniggered. "She is more a man than he, that is for sure," muttered one.

Suddenly Tobias drew back his sword and swept it low at my legs. I saw the move in plenty of time and was able to jump up so that the blade passed harmlessly through the air below me, rather than parting my legs from my body as he intended.

The shame of it for him, was that this move then left his chest exposed.

With a small grin I stepped in and flicked the tip of my blade down from his throat to his knees. My aim was true; this opened the front of his dress without touching his skin, so that it fell open and bared his chest down to his belly. He stepped back; his mouth open but no sound coming out. I then flicked my wrist and knocked his sword from his hand, so it fell onto the rushes with a dull thud.

"I said, do not make yourself a fool," I repeated, holding my blade steady not two inches away from his bare chest, as the room erupted into gales of laughter. I waited a moment, until the noise died down and the room was quiet enough for me to be heard. "Begone, you unpleasant little turncoat," I said, "before I skewer you like a boar upon a spit."

He glanced around at all the men observing this scene, once again roaring with laughter, then back at me, his eyes burning with hatred. I could see he was struggling to hold himself together in the face of such humiliation, then he shook his head, pulled the front of the ripped garment together as if that would restore his dignity, turned and walked towards the door.

The horse was no longer in the way, so he was able to

walk out as steadily as he could, past Sir Reginald and Hal who were leaning on either side of the open door, holding their swords casually by their sides.

The waves of laughter followed him out into the night, and continued for a while after he had gone. I sheathed my sword, keeping an unwavering eye on Sir Reginald, waiting to see what his next move was going to be.

"By Heaven, girl, that was nicely done," said a voice beside me, and I gave a small nod of acknowledgement at the man who had spoken.

"A cup of Rhenish for the girl," called another man, "for both style and bravery!"

A third came up and clapped me on the back. "As like a man as I have ever seen!" he laughed. "And will surely never see the like again!"

More men started to congratulate me, offering drinks and praise for my actions, seeming thankfully to forget what an unnatural sight I presented.

As they crowded round congratulating me, I never let my sight waver from Sir Reginald, still leaning against the door and holding my gaze across the room with a cold, steady smile.

After a while he slowly detached himself from the door frame and reached for a tankard of ale from a passing serving girl. He drained it in one draft, then gave me an exaggerated wink, which I found more scaring than if he were coming after me with his sword. He raised the empty tankard high and brought it down on the nearest table with a loud crash. This he repeated several times, creating a slow, deliberate rhythm.

Such a noise could not be ignored, and soon the room was silent. He had the full attention of every man there.

And the one girl.

"I trust you have enjoyed the little performance put on by this spirited young woman, Mary Fox," he began. "Leaping in like a march hare, then undressing that unfortunate fellow with a display of swordplay that verged on vulgar showmanship." He looked around the room, commanding every man to listen with the authority of his stare. "You may have thought she is to be admired, clothing herself in manly garb and fighting like a man, but let me tell you, good sirs, she is not." He paused. "You may have thought she has been grievously wronged, that she must take such drastic action. But let me assure you that it is not she who has been wronged at all. No, there is one here that has suffered more by her. One who would love her, cherish her and protect her in his arms, yet how has she repaid such love and kindness?" He shook his head in sorrow. "She has behaved unnaturally and she has spurned him."

There was such silence at these words that you could have heard a mouse cough. He glared around the room. "And that man that she has wronged is me, good sirs. It is me."

Some of the men now began to cast sideways glances in my direction, and those closest to me even moved slightly away.

"Indeed," Sir Reginald continued, "she is betrothed to me in marriage, in the eyes of God and as the law allows." Again he paused for effect. "And although I love her with all my heart, she does not return my affection, nor does she look on the prospect of our union with the same joy and anticipation as I." Here he let his voice break a little, and although I knew the emotion was false, his audience seemed to be swayed by it. "Instead, she dresses unnaturally and runs hither and thither about the country, waving a sword about her like a perverse version of a man." There were more glances in my direction, now with some hostility, and further movements away that left me more isolated, like I was standing on a shore as the tide retreats.

"So I ask only that she returns with me to my home in Essex, dresses as befits her station and her sex. Then she will become my ever-loving wife, and no doubt mother to my sons. For I still grieve for the son I lost but a few short weeks ago, and would look to her youth and ripe belly to give me many more in the years to come." He looked around the room. "Who will help me take this woman back, as God and the law intends?"

The men nearest me, who had so recently given such warm congratulations, now scowled and muttered their disapproval.

"You lack grace, young woman," one observed.

"If you were my daughter, I would not allow such behaviour," another growled.

"This man loves you and will cherish you," said a third. "Put down your sword and go with him."

"And if I do not?" I asked of this one, a swarthy yeoman.

"Look about you," he answered. "These men are now on the side of your future husband." He was right; the bearded faces around me radiated disapproval; a sea of scowls, frowns and basilisk stares.

There was no doubt I was now totally on my own.

I bit my lip. Was this how my adventures would conclude – to return once more to Marchington Manor in that cursed cart, crossing the threshold again with my head hung in shame, to be imprisoned in my room and bound into constricting gowns, before being sold off to Sir Reginald in wedlock, like a cut of meat?

My hand found the hilt of my sword and I gripped it hard. Whatever the outcome of this night, it would not end in me climbing back into that cursed cart!

I looked about me again, measuring the distances; taking note of the position of the table beside me; making my plans.

"What say you, Mary?" called Sir Reginald. "Will you come quietly, and return to your true, loving family and our happy wedding?"

I could feel my lip curl in distaste as I stared at him. "Nay, de Courtney," I answered, "for all you say is as false as that smile you wear. If I return with you it will be to a life of servitude and misery, and I will never do so willingly." I paused, looking to see how this was being received by the men around me. Unfortunately, they remained stern and disapproving. "You will have to take me by force. Then these men will see the truth
of my words."

"I thought as much," he said. There was a pause, then he shouted, "Enough of this nonsense! Seize her!"

After that, everything happened fast.

Hal launched himself across the room, as I felt hands grabbing me from behind.

I twisted and dropped to the floor in one movement,

shaking off those trying to hold me, and as Hal arrived with his sword held before him, I quickly stood, then took one step up onto a bench beside me, followed by a jump onto the top of the table.

With a wicked grin, Hal swung his sword at my legs just as Tobias had done before, but I had already leapt upwards and hooked my hands over the oak beam of the roof that crossed above it. Hal's sword passed harmlessly through the air below my feet, nearly beheading the swarthy yeoman.

Hanging from the beam allowed me to pull my legs up behind me, then swing them forward in a vicious kick that caught Hal on the chin, snapping his head back and sending him crashing to the floor. After he had gone down, I swung back again as hard as I could and let go of the beam, so that I flew backwards through the air and cleared the bannister rail of the stairway behind me, landing in a crouch halfway up the stairs.

This move caught all the men by surprise, so I was able to turn and run up to the top floor unchallenged, drawing my sword as I went.

As I turned the corner at the top, I saw Sir Reginald from the side of my eye starting up the stairs behind me.

I ran along the passageway, making for my own room. Once inside, I quickly closed the door and ran to the still open window.

I was just preparing to make the same exit down the blanket as before, when there was a loud crash and I turned to see the door fly open, revealing Sir Reginald.

There was no time to turn my back to him and exit through the window, so I came on guard and faced him.

"Does it come to this, Mary?" he panted. "Must I slay you instead of wed you?"

"If you must," I answered, "for I would prefer that."

"You would rather die than become my bride?" he said. "Am I so truly terrible that you would prefer death to me?"

"You know the truth of that," I answered. "I have already refused an offer of marriage from another, and he is ten times the man you will ever be."

"More fool you, then."

There was a silence as we faced each other, then he nodded, as if confirming to himself what he would now do. "So then I will accede to your wishes, Mary," he said. "I will not now seek to wed you. But," he added, "I will not have my honour so badly used by a mere woman. Your father made his wishes clear. Prepare to die instead."

With that he came at me, his sword flicking left and right many times, as I parried and blocked each move as best I could, watching like a hawk as his blade flashed before me, just as my brothers had taught. He seemed to have limitless energy despite his years, able to keep his sword moving without pause for what seemed like an age, and I felt my wrist and arm start to ache. I knew that I would soon tire and make a fatal error.

He seemed to sense this and doubled his speed, so I must increase the swiftness of my responses in return, or suffer the dreadful consequence.

My arm was soon feeling as if it was on fire, but still I managed to block and parry his advances, as he pushed me back. Suddenly I felt my lower back touch something solid, and I found myself fighting with my legs against the window-sill and my back now in the open air.

He made a feint left and right that I parried as best I could, but this left my centre exposed.

With a triumphant yell he thrust directly at my chest.

Giving a desperate cry I flicked my sword back, managing to turn his blade at the last possible moment. This left our swords locked hilt to hilt, with his close to my face and the two of us almost touching like the lovers we could never be. He fixed me with his cold smile as he used his superior weight and strength to push his blade ever closer, until it was but a hair's breadth from my face and I was close to overbalancing out of the window.

As Sir Reginald pushed me ever further over the sill, I braced myself with my free hand then drove my knee up as hard as I could into his crotch.

With a thin cry like steam escaping from a kettle, he staggered back and fell onto the bed, his hands to his manhood.

For a moment I considered placing my sword to his throat and pushing it in, but I could not kill a man in cold blood – not even Sir Reginald. Instead I went quickly to the window, climbed to the sill, steadied myself and dropped down – onto the roof of the cart that still stood below. I thought I would untether the horse and use it to make good my escape.

But just as I ran along the roof to the driver's seat and grabbed the reins, I heard a crashing sound behind me and felt the cart lurch. I turned to see Sir Reginald crouching after landing on the roof as well.

He shook his head slowly as he stood up. "I had thought you a strange woman, but one I could tame," he said, his voice pitched somewhat higher than its usual growl. "But now I see you are like a wild horse, that simply cannot be broken." He raised his sword. "Such an unworkable beast must be put down. It is the only way."

Then he advanced again, and I found myself once more in a desperate fight.

But this time I had a plan. As he came at me, I used my free hand to pull on the rein behind my back, so the horse was forced round. This meant the cart suddenly swung to one side. Knowing this was coming, my knees were flexed to absorb the movement, but Sir Reginald was caught by surprise. As the cart started to move, he over-balanced, scrabbled desperately for a hold, then rolled off the edge and fell to the ground.

Quickly I gathered both reins and flicked them across the horse's back. The animal completed his turn and started to trot away from the inn and down the lane. I moved into the driver's seat, and flicked the reins again, trying to get enough speed to get away.

But it was not enough.

Almost immediately I heard running footsteps, then Sir Reginald appeared beside me and swung up beside where I was sitting.

I jumped up from the driver's seat and stepped onto the roof as the cart swayed along, my sword held at the ready, my legs wide and my knees flexed to steady myself. He climbed up as well and came after me, his blade once again flashing at me from left, right and centre, so I must do all I could to stop it.

Then we passed out of the pool of light cast from the

braziers outside the inn, and it was suddenly very dark, for the moon was hidden behind a cloud. Sir Reginald checked as the cart swayed violently, and I could just make out that he had dropped to a crouch to stop himself once again falling from the roof.

The moon passed from behind the cloud and I caught sight of what was behind him.

I pointed my sword at him and said, "Get up and fight."

He looked up. "With pleasure."

He stood to his full height, just as the horse trotted under the low trees at the end of the lane.

The first branch caught him in the back of the head, and I could hear the dull cracking sound as it made as it hit, causing him to fall forward and slide off the roof. Immediately I crouched down to avoid the branches myself, and once they had passed harmlessly above me, I scrambled to the driver's seat and pulled the horse up. Then I jumped down from the cart and ran back to his prostrate body lying in the lane.

I crouched beside him, watching for a moment to see if he moved. He remained still, so gingerly I put my fingers to his neck. I could feel the faintest fluttering of his pulse, so he was still alive.

I stood and looked down at his still form.

This man, who had pursued me so hard for so long, had declared he would 'put me down' like horse that could not be broken. I tried to feel some pity for him, but could find none in my heart. I pictured the cold smile, the pleasure he took in describing how ill he would use me as his wife, the casual cruelty to Sir John in the forest, the threats made at Hythe Quay... How could he be worthy of my pity? I shook my head in sorrow. I would leave him to take his chance, for just as in the bedroom earlier, I could not find in my heart to finish him off, even though I once again had him at my mercy.

I looked up. The moon lit up the countryside in a soft blue glow, showing the path ahead winding away under the trees. A path that led to... where? To new possibilities and new adventures...

I went over to the horse and had just started to untether him from the cart, ready to mount him and ride away as quick as possible, when I felt the ground trembling with approaching hoofbeats.

In horror I watched as a ghostly dark figure appeared in the moonlight, galloping towards me from the direction of the inn.

Desperately I fumbled with the traces, but my fingers could not get the knots undone, and the man was upon me, his horse rearing up as he pulled it to a halt.

"Mary Fox?" he called down, and my breath caught as I realised it was not one of my pursuers. Thank the Lord, it was not Hal, Tom or even Tobias!

"Yes?" I answered, relief mixed with caution as to what this stranger who knew my name could possibly want with me.

He leapt down from his horse and swept off his cap, bowing low.

"Marcus Kytson, mistress, at your service."

He stood up and I saw him more clearly in the moonlight. He was tall, maybe a few years older than me, with blonde hair that fell across his forehead and clear eyes above a trim, dark beard.

"Yes, Master Kytson?"

He replaced his cap. "I was in the Sun Inn this evening," he said, "and I saw how well you handled yourself."

I admit I had not seen him, for I am sure I would have recalled his strong face and broad shoulders, but then I suppose I had had other things to occupy my mind at the time.

"From the moment when you swung in past that horse's head, then disrobed that boy with swordplay that few could have mastered as well, then leapt to the roof like an acrobat and dispatched that scoundrel with a kick, before swinging backwards onto the stair – t'was a magnificent display!"

I found myself warming to this Marcus Kytson for the boyish delight he took in my actions. "Thank you, sir, but I was only trying to get away from those who would do me harm." I turned back to the traces and continued to untie the horse.

"So I warrant," he replied. "Then you fought that de Courtney fellow on the roof of this cart and conspired with the horse to dislodge him…" he shook his head and smiled. "'This girl,' I thought to myself, 'is the one I need for my task.'"

The traces came away and the horse was freed. I grasped the reins and turned back to him.

"What task is that?" I asked. "I do not seek a new task."

"But you are perfect," he answered with a small laugh. "Dressed in boy's garb you are perfect in both physique and face for the task."

"You would have me play a role?"

"That I would." He became serious. "My need is most pressing, and I would reward you with a substantial sum of money."

"I am not motivated by money, sir." I pulled myself up onto the horse and settled on his back.

"No?" He also swung into his saddle, and we faced each other in the moonlight. "But money can buy you freedom, for a woman of means has more choices as to how to live her life." He paused. "I am offering a hundred sovereigns."

I looked up at the clouds thudding across the night sky. A hundred sovereigns! True, a woman was always the property of a man – her father then her husband – but with that kind of money I could set up home for myself. Or I could stay on the move, able to pay my way with ease as I went about the country…

"What would I need to do for that?" I enquired.

"I have a friend who has a son, and he has gone missing," he answered.

"And you want me to find him?"

"No, I want you to pretend to be him, for a visit by his father."

"You would offer me a hundred sovereigns to fool this boy's father that I am his son?" I asked. "Would the father not know his own son?"

"Not this father. The boy was born out of wedlock, and he has not seen his son more than once or twice since he was a babe."

"So the boy is a bastard. Then why is the visit so important?"

"Because of who the father happens to be. And because he is considering making the boy his legitimate heir."

I paused. Should I take this further? Or should I just ride

away now and make my own adventures? I will admit, I was intrigued…

"And this boy's name?"

"Henry Fitzroy, son of Elizabeth Blount.

"And his father?" I needed to hear it said, although I fancy I already knew.

"His father is King Henry the Eighth."

The moon shone down on his expectant face. "Will you do it, Mary Fox?" he asked. "Will you be the Tudor Prince for me?"

I smiled.

"Yes, Master Kytson," I said. "Yes, I will."

THE END

Mary will return soon in her new adventure:
THE TUDOR PRINCE

About the Author

Jonathan Posner is a novelist based in the UK, with a passion for the action and adventure to be found in Tudor England.

He has always been captivated by Tudor history, and has also been a lifelong fan of action-adventure novels. So when he decided in 2015 to write a novel himself, it had to be the kind of adventure he loves to read; one with plenty of action, danger and suspense. And, of course it had to be set in Tudor England, with a time-travelling heroine finding herself thrown into the deep end of this fascinating historical era.

The result was **The Witchfinder's Well**, part 1 of a trilogy. **The Alchemist's Arms** (part 2) followed in 2019 and part 3, **The Sovereign's Secret**, in Summer 2022.

This book - **The Broken Sword** - is the first of a series of adventures featuring an unconventional Tudor heroine called Mary Fox. More books about Mary's adventures are also planned.

Jonathan's other works include a book of short stories called

Once Upon an Ending, a one-act play called **Private Eyes**, as well as book and lyrics for three Musicals - **Spirit of History** which premiered in Old Windsor, **Hot, Mean & Green**, which premiered at the Rhoda McGaw Theatre in Woking, and **A Fine Time for Wine**, which also premiered in Old Windsor.

Jonathan is the father of two adult sons and lives in Exeter, UK. When not writing he is a regular presenter on local radio.

For more information and to sign up for Jonathan's regular newsletter, please visit Jonathan's author website
jonathanposnerauthor.com.

Jonathan's books are published by
Winter & Drew Publishing
winteranddrew.com

By the Same Author

If you have enjoyed Mary Fox's adventure, you may also enjoy another Tudor-era series by Jonathan Posner. It tells the story of Justine Parker, a modern-day girl who time travels back to Tudor England and becomes a celebrated adventurer.

The first book in the series is **The Witchfinder's Well**. It tells how Justine (inspired by the Mary Fox adventures!) time-travels from 2015 to 1565 and outwits a sinister witchfinder to become Lady Mary de Beauvais.

Readers have said:

"A must for everyone who loves history and a must for everyone who wants to be whisked away to another time."

"An enchanting and un-put-downable read!"

"A good tale, entertaining, funny, informative, recommended, a good holiday book, one to go back to again and again."

The second book is **The Alchemist's Arms**, which picks the story up a few years later. A time-travelling assassin has Queen Elizabeth in his sights. Can Lady Mary stop him?

The third book is called **The Sovereign's Secret**. Lady Mary's past catches up with her, putting her in dreadful danger. Can she avoid her fate, and in doing so, will she change history forever?

SEARCH ALL TITLES ON AMAZON
OR ORDER FROM YOUR LOCAL BOOKSHOP

For further information go to Jonathan's website.
jonathanposnerauthor.com